PEOPLE WHO NEED TO DIE

Short Stories

By Victor Rook

A Rook Communications Publication

Publisher Information:
Rook Communications
P.O. Box 571
Manassas, VA 20108

Email: vic@victorrook.com

Website:
Go to victorrook.com to order books and DVDs by Victor Rook.

ISBN 10: 0-9766653-5-2
ISBN 13: 978-0-9766653-5-9

Cover Design: Victor Rook

For a better world.

Dedicated to all the people who put up with idiots every day.
May these stories bring you laughter and solace.

Table of Contents

Introduction

The year is 2021 and people are fed up. Resources have been depleted, the environment is in shambles, and current population growth has become unsustainable. The governments of the World Order Alliance concluded that in order to reestablish a peaceful and prosperous society, thirty percent of the population must go.

First eradicated were the already imprisoned—the murderers, the rapists, the robbers, and the sex offenders—through a two-month mass-execution spectacle. The televised event recouped nearly forty billion dollars to the world economies, but only one percent of the population was eliminated.

When the order came down to control the population through "selective" homicides, Earth's inhabitants could barely contain their excitement. Bloodlust for those who do evil, or who just pissed people off, had been brewing for decades.

Each murder required an application stating the reason and method for removal. Once the application was processed and approved, the perpetrator had one year to carry out the crime.

These are the unlucky targets.

Bad Drivers

Outside of her screams, the only sound was the flutter from passing support posts as her 2019 Honda Prelude sped along the metal guardrail at ninety miles per hour. Beyond the guardrail lay the majestic Ocklawaha River, which snaked through the countryside like one of those large, invasive pythons. It would have been a pretty sight, if it weren't all a blur.

Her brakes had stopped functioning twenty miles back, just after leaving the motel and moments after the incident at the traffic light on Mathis. Next, the steering wheel wrenched from her tight grip and abruptly turned the car left on Saguaro Drive, where she had intended to turn right. The accelerator pedal sank below the sole of her toeless white pump, racing her car onto Florida's Highway 33 a mile later.

Teresa Hollinbeck was her name, or *is* her name—IS being a temporary situation—the former school secretary at Fairview High who was fired three months earlier for stealing office supplies. Not just a pen or pad here and there, but boxes of paper, toner, a large printer, and even a new laptop. She had wanted them for her side career as an independent realtor. Security cameras captured her thievery during prom night.

Her life quickly spun out of control, much like the situation she currently found herself in. Her husband filed for divorce when he found out she had been cheating on him with one of her clients. That's where she was earlier this day, spending time with bearded Rob Sanders at the Waverly Inn. Rob was hoping to convince her to move into the new waterfront cottage he planned on buying; she was hoping to get him to sign on the dotted line so she could afford next month's rent.

Now she was alone with her car holding her hostage as it flew along Highway 33 at breakneck speed. The 911 recording went something like this:

"Hello, 911. What is your location and emergency?"

"I'm on Highway 33 and my car won't stop!"

"What do you mean your car won't stop?"

"It won't stop. The brakes won't work."

"Can you switch the car into neutral?"

"I tried, but the lever seems to be stuck!"

"What happens when you take your foot off the accelerator?"

"Nothing, it just stays there!"

"Is it caught on something? The pedal?"

"No, it won't lift up either."

"What part of Highway 33 are you on? Can you see any exit signs?"

"I don't know. It's going too fast."

"Are there other cars around you?"

"Yes, a few. The car, my car, steers around them." (panting sounds)

"What do you mean your car steers around them. Are *you* steering around them?"

"No, it's doing it on its own!"

That's when a male voice came over the car's GPS speaker.

"You've been tagged."

The phone connection went dead a moment later, and Teresa

found herself begging and praying for the car to stop. Her prayers were answered two miles later when the vehicle slipped through an opening in the guardrail past mile marker 45 and plunged into Green Swamp. Everything inside shuffled around upon impact. A few pens impaled the interior roof and stuck there like darts. A warm stream of blood trickled down the bridge of her nose and over her lips. She had hit her head on the steering wheel, but was still conscious enough to see where she had landed.

The car floated on the surface for a minute or two, and in that time she thought about the rides at Epcot, the Maelstrom in particular, which sent you through a maze of waterways. It felt like that—bouncy and random, out of your control, yet safe enough that you knew it would eventually deliver you to the other side. But there was no other side, in this case. There was only down.

At first the water seeped in slowly through the vents and around the rubber seals at the base of the doors. Her feet sloshed around in a puddle already four inches deep when she attempted to open the driver-side door. It wouldn't budge. The locks were frozen, as if the entire electrical system had collapsed, though she could still see the lit screen on the built-in GPS. Her seat belt held her firmly in place, too. It wouldn't unclasp.

On the floor, just within reach, was one of the toner cartridges she had stolen. She grasped it with her right hand and banged the blunt end repeatedly against the window. The tempered glass held strong, as if it were fighting back. Then all the car windows did something unusual—they rolled down half way. By now the rancid water was up to her waist, sloshing between her thighs and splashing onto her chest. Panic-stricken, she cried out for help several times.

"You've been tagged" repeated louder through the GPS speaker, making her think that someone had heard her pleas and had come to her rescue. But there was no one around for miles.

Then the car tilted to its side, causing the water to cascade over top of the partially opened windows. Seconds later it was as if she were in the center of a waterfall, the murky green water filling the car from all sides as the car leveled out and began to sink. The water was at her neck when she let out her final terrified screams. Her last inhale was met with a clump of algae, which lodged within her throat and deprived her of any hopeful, sustaining breath. The car quickly disappeared below the surface after the windows opened the rest of the way on their own.

Bubbles turned to splashes as gators left the shore to explore the hand-delivered meal.

Investigators pulled the wreckage from Green Swamp two weeks later, hours after George Stillman reeled into his rowboat a white shoe with a decaying foot inside. He thought he had snagged the biggest largemouth bass ever recorded in Polk County. The rest of Teresa's body couldn't be found, though fragments of her shredded blouse and jeans were detected inside a pile of droppings along the shore a dozen yards from the wreckage. The sated gators basked in the sun—their roving eyes gleaming like children hoping to lick the bowl—while the car was hoisted out of the water and placed onto a flatbed truck.

Without a body, forensics couldn't perform a toxicology report. In reviewing the 911 recording, investigators weren't sure if Ms. Hollinbeck, as she was now referred to, was under the influence of alcohol or any other drugs. The bartender from Joe's Good Times Tavern, which sat around the corner from the Waverly Inn, recognized the picture of Teresa the cops presented to her. The last credit card purchase Teresa made led them to the drinking hole.

"Yeah, she was in here. She was with some guy with a beard, I think." When asked if they had drank a lot on the night before the accident, Pamela gave the same answer she gave to anyone who questioned the sobriety of their patrons: "Everyone has a good time at Joe's Good Times Tavern."

There was speculation that Teresa's call may have been a stunt to conceal from family and friends that she was intending to take her own life. Investigators had drudged up the report on her school thefts, of which charges were dropped because she claimed she was using the items to work on school matters from home. Ron, the bearded client, confessed to being with Teresa the morning of the accident. Detailed records of his whereabouts, including receipts at a gas station across town during the time of Teresa's 911 call, supported his innocence in the matter.

Mechanics were unable to detect any problems with Teresa's car. Locals questioned why it took investigators two weeks to pinpoint the accident, since after 2017 all cars were required to have a built-in GPS locator. They came standard on new cars; others required retrofitting. However, it was still being contested in courts on whether auto manufacturers should be required to allow tracking information to be turned over to investigative officials. Only if a crime had been committed and a warrant issued were they required to do so. New car owners rejected the new technology over privacy concerns, and manufacturers knew it could lead to lost sales. At the time of the accident, Teresa also had her cell phone's GPS switched off.

Teresa's death was listed as an accident, and the 911 recording was stored away at the Polk County Dispatch Center. Investigators assumed that the faint male voice, which they believed said, "You've been wagged," (wagging being a new dance craze similar to twerking) had come from the car radio.

Until it happened again.

Ricky Fulwell left the Lake County Fair in his 2016 Chevy pickup with a bottle of Coors nestled between his thighs. Once he hit State Road 19, he pulled the bottle up to his lips for a long sip, then held it against the steering wheel with his right hand. This was his eighth, maybe tenth, since seeing Jessie at the event with Carl Baker. For the past two hours he had watched her laugh, flip her hair from side to side, and hold hands with that douchebag. He had concealed himself within the fold of the sizable crowd. That bitch moves a little too fast, he thought. It had been less than two weeks since they stopped seeing each other.

Traffic on the road was slower than usual that Saturday night. Out of frustration he unrolled his window and stuck his arm out to tap on the truck's roof. Beads of sweat dripped off his forehead and moistened his unkempt stubble. Reflections from the taillights of the car ahead of him illuminated his glazed eyes, which swirled within a fiery rage. He replayed her night's betrayal in his head over and over again. Seeing her kiss Carl on the lips had sent him into one of his episodes, no doubt the reason for their breakup in the first place.

"You fucking whore!" is what he shouted before kicking over a trash can next to a funnel cake stand and stumbling back to his truck in the dark, adjacent field. His tires ripped into the dirt exit lane, sending a cloud of smoke over to the ticket booth where a final band of teenagers waited to get inside. The rubber screeched when it hit the pavement, and now he was already fifteen miles away.

"Move! What the fuck!" Ricky edged his truck closer to the car ahead of him. He wanted to get to Carl's place before midnight, closing time for the fair. He knew he'd bring her back there, and he had a plan for both of them.

"God dammit! Fuckin' traffic." He pulled the beer back up to his mouth and swigged the last half of it all at once. A trickle of foam spilled down his chin and onto his soiled gray T-shirt. The woman in the car beside him pointed and looked back to her husband.

"What the fuck you lookin' at?" Ricky tossed the empty bottle to the passenger floor where it clanked against the others. The onlookers sped up, apparently jarred by the noise. *Maybe the guy has a gun.* Ricky swerved into the left lane and followed close behind.

"C'mon, fuckers. You wanna play with me?" He gained on them within moments, forcing them over to the right lane. Next it was a blue sedan in the way, and although they were traveling at the speed limit, Ricky crept the front of his truck within feet of the car's back bumper. "Slow shitheads! Move the FUCK out of my way!"

This went on for a couple more minutes, Ricky displacing half a dozen more drivers in that time. He was reaching into the back seat for another Coors when his GPS spoke out.

"You've been tagged."

"What? Who said that?" He popped the cap off the new bottle and flipped it out the window while looking side to side. "Shit, must be in my head." He laughed. "That's what I'll tell that bastard Carl. You've been tagged, mother fucker."

He laid his arm back out the window, steering with the other, when his truck abruptly returned to the right lane on its own. Before he could grab the wheel with both hands, the truck's windows charged upward, trapping his one arm at the elbow. He struggled to pull it free, spilling the open beer over his lap and drenching the crotch of his shorts in the process. It wouldn't budge. The buttons on the door's armrest seemed to be jammed as well.

"Jesus Christ! Mother Fuck!"

The truck slowed as it approached the exit for Pilner Road, where it left the highway. Pilner was an old country road that went on for miles without much of anything but trailers on cinder blocks surrounded by knee-high weeds. It was a humid night, and the mosquitoes were out in full force. A swarm of them began feasting on his exposed arm. The truck crawled at twenty miles per hour in near pitch darkness while he pounded the window with his other hand until his knuckles bled.

"Open, god dammit. Open!"

Five minutes later the truck slowed to a stop at the dimly lit intersection of Pilner and Washner Roads. Below the Washner

7

post was a crusty triangular sign with the words "Waste Management" surrounded by a thick white border. The truck turned onto Washner and quickly picked up speed.

"Stop! Dammit!" Ricky punched the brakes with both feet with no effect. He strained his free arm toward his cell phone, which had fallen to the passenger floor, but his reach fell just inches short. He popped his right foot out of his flip-flop and swung his leg over the center console. His toes fumbled through the wet bottles while he tried to grasp the phone with them.

Outside, his left arm swelled from the numerous bug bites. Large welts oozed tiny red droplets. He would do anything to scratch it, but that was his least concern right now. The truck had made its way all four miles down Washner, which dead-ended at the Lake County Landfill. A series of left and right turns had maneuvered him close to the landfill entrance gate. There was a narrow gap in the chain-link fence. The truck idled about twenty yards in front of the opening when Ricky finally managed to clench the phone between his big toe and index toe. He quickly pulled it up into his right hand. As he dialed 911, the engine revved to full throttle.

The truck rushed toward the narrow opening as fast as Ricky had sped out of the fairgrounds less than an hour before. The 911 operator clicked in just in time to hear his agonizing screams. His trapped arm had whacked into the left gatepost and torn off. It swung from a loose wire like a pendulum before falling to the ground. *Thump.* Inside the truck the GPS voice repeated, as if to mark the dismemberment, "You've been tagged." Seconds later the truck collided with the two-foot-high cement barrier surrounding the landfill, sending it end over end down the deep embankment where it crashed into a pile of city waste. A wooden broom handle shot through the windshield and impaled Ricky's head through his mouth. The dislodged GPS unit, which dangled inches from his face, issued its parting call.

"Trash delivery."

Ricky's bloated corpse was discovered three days later after Clyde, a neighborhood mutt, was found chewing on the severed arm on his owner's back porch. Half of Ricky's face had been pecked away, most likely by the large black vultures that spent much of the day hovering over the landfill, assumed investigators. When Polk County Sheriff, James Dennis, got word of the cryptic "You've been tagged" recording from the evening news, he opened up an investigation between the neighboring counties. Ricky's death was eventually ruled an accident caused by drunk driving, as his blood alcohol level was estimated to be five times the legal limit. The woman who spotted him on the highway also came forward when she saw his picture. She described in detail his drinking and aggressive driving that night.

"I thought that man was out of his mind!" she said to the WTOC reporter.

Susan Walker, one of many in Polk and Lake Counties following the story, felt that the tragic accidents over the past two weeks were like something out of a horror movie.

"That poor woman, drowning inside her car while being eaten by alligators. And now this man driving himself into a landfill. I don't know what's gotten into people these days."

Her fourteen-year-old stepson, Shane Walker, thought differently. He watched the news with morbid fascination. Not in front of his family during dinnertime, of course, but when the story repeated on the eleven o'clock news. He set his DVR to record it, then watched it over and over again as if he were performing his own investigation.

Shane was a smart but quiet kid who spent much of his time locked away in his room playing video games. He had recently taken up photography, as his new smartphone was able to capture detailed images at fifty megapixels. *At least this gets you out of the house*, his stepmother would say. He manipulated one of those images that night after his parents went to bed. Zoomed in it looked like a blur of red and gray pixels. When resized to fit the screen, it was readily apparent what it was: a pickup truck sitting in the parking lot of the Waverly Inn.

Shane returned to the motel the following day and sat on the concrete base of the motel sign. It was the perfect spot to take pictures of cars passing in front along Mathis Road. Next he biked across town and captured images of vehicles entering and leaving the Waverly Outlet Mall. When a blue Chrysler minivan rounded the corner at the mall's entrance, he was reminded of the van his mother used to drive him to school in. Sometimes she and his dad would take him and his little sister, Sherri, on long day trips in it. Once they used it to camp for a weekend in the Osceola National Forest near Lake City. He missed her very much.

"This is for you, mom," he said, as he snapped the last car photo of the day: a white 2019 Toyota Prius. That would make three hundred total. Not a bad start.

The Prius belonged to Ashley Anderson, a junior at Florida State University currently on summer break. Or, she would have been a junior, had she not *Graumanned* herself into the cement parking lot on the corner of Tremont and Jackson a week later.

On that fateful Friday night, she had joined two of her friends from Alpha Delta Pi for a mid-break gathering. The plan was to hit all three of their favorite hangouts by midnight: Sierra Cafe, Hard Rock, and Club Nitro. Each girl had driven her own car in case she got lucky with the local frat boys, who were also perusing the scene. While traveling between hot spots, they texted and talked back and forth.

"I can't believe Danny is in town. That guy was a creep to Julia." Ashley laughed while steering her Prius with one hand and talking with the other. Her tires repeatedly crossed over the center line. "I hope he doesn't make it to Nitro." A passing driver glared at her. "What?" She laughed again and ran her fingers through her shoulder-length hair. "I don't know. About five inches. Ha ha. Trust me, there isn't much upstairs *or* downstairs."

Following close behind were Tina and Selma, who shared in the three-way conversation. "Do you think Sandy will show up?" Tina asked.

"Oh, I hope not. Remember what she wore last time? I don't know *how* she got into our sorority. Sister needs to lower that skirt a bit." Selma was third in the line of cars.

"Skank. Skankity skank." Ashley laughed so hard she almost dropped her phone. Her abrupt left turn onto Paloma Avenue immediately after nearly clipped the front end of the car waiting at the light. Three seconds later her Prius lunged forward.

"You've been tagged."

"Ashley, where are you going?" Tina struggled to catch up.

"I don't know. Something's wrong with my car." Ashley pumped the brakes. "It won't slow down."

"Stop playing with us. It's hard to catch up." Selma just made the light at Norton Street.

"Slow down, sister!"

"I can't! It won't let me!" By now Ashley was three blocks ahead of her friends, far enough away that they didn't see her car turn down Tremont Avenue. Tremont led to a new industrial park at the edge of town.

"Ashley? Ashley?"

"Where are you?"

A dead spot between a line of buildings cut off Ashley's cell signal. Her arms ached from trying to gain control of the steering wheel, but her car wouldn't have it. When the locks shot down and her seat belt tightened, she screamed at the top of her lungs. It had the piercing shrill of the blonde bimbo in a slasher film who is always first or second to die.

The surrounding lighting waned as the car approached the new J. Gibson building, which would house their Southeast corporate offices. It was nearly pitch black when her Prius rammed through a line of orange cones and into the structure's freshly paved parking lot. Night workers had completed the project less than an hour before. Once the car bogged to a halt, the door locks popped open and the seat belt unclasped.

Ashley abruptly grabbed her phone and jumped out of the car. What she didn't see in the darkness, as she lumbered through her final steps, was the stray pylon in her path. The toe of her left foot, already caked with a heavy gob of cement, caught the edge and sent her face first into the wet mortar. The fall knocked her out cold. Her phone landed upright in the cement three feet away. The last number dialed.

"Ashley? Where are you? This isn't funny. I am *so* not liking this. You better not make us late. Anyway, ciao."

It took a jackhammer and five guys to exhume Ashley from the hardened cement the next day. She was found face down and spread eagle, like an upside-down snow angel. The gray "snow" had completely extracted the moisture from her face, hands, and feet, locking her into the imprint. As they carried the concrete slab away with her body still attached, Shane snapped pictures from across the street. When the flatbed truck rushed to the morgue, Ashley's long hair fluttered in the wind like the mane of a well-preserved fossil.

Her car was towed to an impound lot where it was later retrieved as evidence. When asked if there was anything unusual about her final conversation with Ashley, Tina recalled the male voice and its foreboding alert. Sheriff Dennis jumped on the case.

Could this be another Toyota scandal on the rise, he thought. Back in 2009, several Toyota owners died after reporting their vehicles accelerating on their own. After a large recall of affected models, in which Toyota claimed it was a problem with the floor mats, the company finally conceded that another cause was defective gas pedals. But this was happening with several different manufacturers: Honda, GM, and now a Toyota.

A few rubbernecks who witnessed Ashley being taken away remembered seeing a young man at the site with his smartphone. Others were taking pictures, too, but the kid seemed intent on documenting every angle and facet of the scene, including the vehicle. Sheriff Dennis shrugged it off as par for the gore-obsessed youth culture.

In his darkened bedroom, Shane transferred Ashley's pictures to a folder labeled "Completed." Then he called up the car photos he took earlier in the week and began digitizing them into computer-generated replicas. Once he finished a specific model, like a 2018 Chrysler Voyager, changing the color was as simple as clicking a button. He only needed one picture of each model, and if that model hadn't changed much in appearance from year to year, all the better.

On his second monitor he watched small green squares move about an intricate green grid. Waiting.

The next two victims, a man and a woman, crashed into each other head on. Side-by-side 911 dispatchers realized they had a potential problem when both drivers reported their cars accelerating on the same road: Calvert Avenue. One was headed northbound; the other, south. Before the operators could verbally guide them away from each other—it really wouldn't have mattered since they had no control over their vehicles anyway— the van and sedan impacted. Both drivers exited through their windshields as if they had been shot out of cannons, their bodies colliding mid-air. It took coroners two hours to peel them apart. Their mangled limbs intertwined, bone around bone, muscle around muscle. Their jaws locked into each other like conjoined rings. It was one of the most gruesome, yet somehow, strangely erotic aftermaths of any accident scene.

"What's your name, son?" Sheriff Dennis approached Shane, who hid behind a tree on the opposite side of the road.

"Shane. It's Shane."

"What are you taking pictures for?"

"I don't know. I guess I'm trying to figure out why all these accidents are happening. Have you figured it out?"

"No, son. But we're trying." Sheriff Dennis paused and placed his hand on Shane's shoulder. "This really isn't something someone as young as you should be seeing. Why don't you let us handle this? You go on now and bike somewhere. It's a nice day out. A young man like yourself should be having fun."

"OK, officer. I'll do that." Shane tucked his smartphone back into his pocket and lifted his bike up from the sidewalk. At the edge of the block he stopped and looked back. Sheriff Dennis had kneeled down and was inspecting the underside of the van. Shane pulled out his phone and quickly snapped an image of his patrol car—a Ford Taurus Interceptor, which replaced the Crown Victoria as the cop car of choice back in 2012. It would be an easy add.

Back at the crime lab, Sheriff Dennis reviewed the male voice recordings. No similar DNA was found at the different accident scenes, which ruled out that another person had been in the cars with the victims. The wave pattern in gator Teresa and landfill Ricky's recordings matched that of the recent accident almost exactly. This suggested that the voice was most likely a pre-recording. Internet searches of "You've been tagged" just came up with old Facebook feature descriptions—nothing conclusive.

Auto manufacturers were mostly hush on the accidents, stating only that the evidence in all cases pointed to driver negligence and driver impairment. It wasn't their fault that Ms. Anderson chose to walk onto fresh cement. And Ms. Hollinbeck and Mr. Fulwell probably *were* attempting suicide. As for the man and the woman who merged together into a single flesh ball, reports showed that recent construction on Calvert Avenue had resulted in a few other accidents and close calls that month.

It wasn't until August 14, 2021, when the next death occurred, and it jarred the entire community.

Juan Remerez drove his 2018 souped-up black Camaro GTX around the parking lot of the Auburndale Walmart Supercenter. In a plastic bag next to him was a bottle of ChromeShine for his $300 rims, the new Purgatory album, "Burn, Fucka, Burn," and a BlastUp energy drink. He had arrived at the store twenty minutes before. Lucky for him there was one open spot close to the entrance. When the other waiting driver (who had been there first) flicked on his signal, Juan punched his accelerator and overtook the spot anyway.

"Gotta be quicker, bro," he mouthed from behind his closed window. He smiled and stroked his chin stubble with his index finger like some sort of victory sign.

Now he was heading down Sawyer Street with Purgatory blasting inside. The car throbbed as if it were the speaker itself. Uncomfortable drivers who happened to be in his path were glad he kept his windows up, at least. With the outside temperature a sweltering ninety-seven degrees this day, air conditioning was a must. He positioned the vent louvers toward his heated scalp before opening the can of BlastUp.

"Fucka, you be roamin', no? Ain't got time, baby, no time for ya, ho!" He pounded the edge of the steering wheel as he rapped along. *"Burn, Fucka, Burn."* Without hesitation he sped through the light at the next intersection right after it turned red. A crossing green sedan slammed on its brakes just in time.

"My pad is rockin' rad, and you be glad, for what you had. But you don't no mo. Burn, Fucka, Burn."

A few miles up he abruptly switched from the left lane to the right without using his turning signal, causing one car to swerve toward the curb, and the one behind it to slam on its brakes.

"Yo man, I'm hungry," he mouthed. He proceeded to the Taco Bell drive-through on Lordes Street.

"Welcome to Taco Bell, how may I help you?"

"Uh, yeah. Hit me up with a Burrito Giganta. Make that two Burrito Gigantas. And, uh, a large Pepsi. And some Cinnamon Twists."

"Will that complete your order."

"Yeh."

"OK, please pull around."

"You've been tagged."

Juan was flipping through a wad of ten-dollar bills when the familiar message emerged from his GPS speaker. He had remembered hearing it on the evening news, but it didn't fully register until his Camaro jerked forward a couple of times and the driver's window closed shut. He pounded on the window and tried the locks, but it was too late. As his car abruptly sped past the payment window, he pressed his face up against his like a child who had just been abducted. Taco Bell employees later recalled the resigned and panicked look.

This time the GPS spoke again.

"Like my ride?"

"Don't take my car, man. Not my car!" Juan's cries were a switch from his overconfident, machismo persona minutes earlier. Yet for the entire trip to the Ratford Center across town, his pleas were answered. The car followed traffic at normal speed, never ran into anything, and never sped onto the nearby highway to deliver him to some remote, hard-to-find location as he had seen on the news. He actually started to enjoy the experience.

"Man, this is trippin'. Where ya takin' me?"

The GPS remained silent, but the seat belts tightened.

At approximately 1:00 p.m., investigators estimated, the car parked itself in the south lot of the Ratford Building. In the Magnifying Glass section, to be exact. It got that name because every afternoon the mirrored glass panels on the side of the tall, concave building focused an intense beam of light onto four specific parking spots: #43-#46. Employees knew not to park there unless they wanted molten car interiors. Juan's Camaro came to rest in space #44. And so did he.

Moments later the air conditioning unit switched over to full heat. Juan tried frantically to close off all the vents, but the rush of hot air percolated through. Sweat oozed from every pore of his body until there was no water left inside him. He downed the sugary, caffeine-boosted can of BlastUp, which dehydrated him further. It didn't help that the car was black, making it absorb the outside rays even faster.

Then the music player cranked up to full volume, forcing him to cover his ears with both hands. "Burn, Fucka, Burn" repeated over and over through the speakers as the temperature inside rose to a scorching one hundred fifty degrees. Just before he passed out he detected the peculiar odor of overripe bananas. That's the smell of human flesh cooking, he recalled from some TV cannibal documentary. He looked down and watched his left arm begin to smoke as his swan song sang him out:

"Burn, Fucka, Burn! Burn, Fucka, Burn! Don't need you no mo. Burn, Fucka, Burn!"

A photo of Juan's charred remains quickly circulated around the Internet. The image showed a blackened man frozen upright in the driver's seat of his car with his fried hands molded to his ears. His roasted red eyeballs hung from their sockets by thin strands. Sizzled black hair twisted in all directions like wood splinters in a fire. It looked like a horror version of Edvard Munch's painting, *The Scream*. "Man Cooked in Car," "Hot Man in Hot Rod," and "Man Leaves Taco Bell for Burning Hell," were the news headlines. This was the kind of attention Polk County didn't want.

Federal Investigators offered a $100,000 reward for the perpetrator of the heinous deaths. Sheriff Dennis continued his own investigation, speculating that the person who posted the photo of Juan's corpse on the Internet could be responsible. Only a few within the Polk County Crime Division had access to the photos taken at the scene once officers arrived. But none of those pictures matched the one leaked. It had to be someone there beforehand. Perhaps an employee within the Ratford Building? But there were hundreds, if not more. It could have been anyone, really. It happened on a Saturday, and kids often used the lot for skateboarding and other activities. When questioned, none of them were even aware that a man had died there days before.

The Sheriff's wife, Lucinda Dennis, witnessed the effects of the case on her husband first-hand. The people in the community wanted answers, and all he could say was that they were "actively working on it." At home at night he would peruse the Internet for hours for any clue. Why were these particular people targeted? What was their connection? Could he predict when it would happen next? Who would be the next driver "tagged"? He hadn't been this frazzled since the accident six years back, the one that devastated him to the point of tears. All she could do was comfort him in the way that she did back then: gently rub his head and shoulders until he was ready for bed.

Shane would lie about his age. The application required that you be 18 or older. But, they wouldn't check. He knew this, just as he knew so much more about how the system worked. They just wanted results, and he was ready to give it to them. He already had. Six and counting.

Polk County got a respite for the next week. There were no more driver fatalities. The same couldn't be said for neighboring Lake and Osceola Counties, however. Four vehicles were pulled from Lake Kissimmee in two days alone. All had the telltale signs of being tagged: 911 calls or onlookers catching sight of the stunned drivers.

Sheriff Dennis felt helpless when he got word; these cases were outside his jurisdiction. All he could do was share the information he had recovered from the Polk County investigations. For the next few days he meandered up and down county streets hoping to make sense of it all. When he approached the Waverly Inn on Mathis, he spotted Shane sitting in his usual place taking pictures of passing cars. He pulled his patrol car into the parking lot and casually walked over to the kid.

"Weren't you that boy I spoke to the other day, the one taking pictures at the Calvert Street accident?"

Shane was surprised to see the officer again. *How would he handle him this time?*

"Yeah, I was there."

"Well, may I ask what you're doing here, right now?"

"Just watching traffic go by."

"C'mon now, I saw your smartphone out when I approached. What are you taking pictures of?"

"Just cars, trucks, different vehicles. There's nothing wrong with that, is there?"

"No, not specifically. But it has me a bit concerned." The officer propped his leg up on the cement base and leaned into Shane, hoping to intimidate him. "You weren't the one who posted that picture on the Internet, were you? The one of the man who died in the Ratford Center parking lot last week?"

"You mean the guy that fried to a crisp? Nah, not me."

"What do you think about that, about all these unexplained accidents?"

"I don't know."

"Well, you must think *something* about them. That sorority girl that got stuck in the cement. Did you take pictures of her, too?"

"What girl?"

"You know who I'm talking about. Some bystanders described you taking pictures of her and the vehicle she drove."

"I don't remember."

"You don't remember." The Sheriff reached out his hand. "Let me see your phone."

"Why?"

"Just let me see your phone. If you have nothing to hide it won't be a big deal."

"I don't have to give you my phone. I've done nothing wrong."

"Well, actually, you *do* have to give me the phone." The Sheriff was right. Back in 2014 the Supreme Court reviewed whether officers could search without a warrant the smartphones of those they arrested. As with all diminishing privacies, not only did they eventually approve the searches, but they also allowed the same if there was "suspicion" that someone had committed a crime. In other words, you didn't have to be arrested to have your on-person belongings seized and examined.

"When do I get it back? I need it for a project I'm working on." Shane reluctantly handed the officer his phone.

"Let me take it down to the station and look at it. Could be a couple of days. You got your address you can give me?"

"It's 8343 Willow Run Circle." The Sheriff scribbled it down in a small notebook.

"And what's your full name, son."

"Shane. Shane Walker."

"OK, Shane. I'm giving you this receipt to let you know that we have your phone. If we find nothing, you'll get it back as soon as possible."

Shane grabbed the piece of paper and walked over to his bike, which he had chained to a rusty lamp pole. The officer returned to his patrol car, slipped the phone inside a small plastic bag, and sped out of the parking lot. Once the Sheriff was out of sight, Shane bolted down Mathis on his ten-speed until he reached Old Folton Road, which was the quickest route back to his house. If the Sheriff returned directly to headquarters, he figured he had twenty minutes to spare, if that.

Sheriff Dennis had something on his mind, a sort of nagging

feeling that something was amiss with that boy. He seemed kind and fairly well mannered, as much as could be expected from a teenager. Maybe it wasn't right to take away his phone with so little evidence. But then again, why would this kid end up at each accident scene before he did? That $100,000 reward would come in handy.

Shane swerved around the intersection of Old Folton and Willow Run Circle. A minute later he skidded into his driveway—nearly crashing into the mailbox in the process—before hopping off his bike just feet from the front steps. His stepmother and father had left for the afternoon to take his little sister fall school shopping, so he would be alone. Inside his bedroom, buttons flicked on and fans whirled as he powered up his computer console and readied for another run. Once the program loaded, he typed in the license number. The monitor with the moving green squares instantly panned over to Jackson Street. Two clicks later a 3D version of the Sheriff's car appeared on the screen.

"You've been tagged."

Sheriff Dennis was less than fifty feet from the entrance to the Polk County Crime Division Headquarters when he heard the familiar message coming from his GPS speaker. This time he wasn't analyzing a recording. The patrol car's locks shot down, the seal belts tightened, and the accelerator pedal dropped to the floor. His head snapped back with the sudden exertion of speed. It was as if the car was just released from a tightly stretched slingshot. It sped past the station entrance and raced for several blocks, then turned right onto the freeway.

He would toy with him a bit. Shane grabbed his tablet controller and tilted it from side to side. As he did, the Sheriff's car zigzagged left and right within the passing lane.

"Stop this! Who are you?"

Shane pressed an up arrow and the patrol car surged from forty to seventy miles per hour in an open section of road.

Another button abruptly slowed it back down to twenty-five. He tilted the tablet back and forth again. The Sheriff's hot coffee swished around and splashed over the rim.

"Who are you? I demand that you tell me who you are!"

Shane ignored the audio coming from his speakers. At least for now. He clicked open a program tab labeled "Instrument Panel" and unchecked A/C. The blower inside the Sheriff's car immediately went silent. It wasn't quite time yet—the sun wasn't in the correct spot—but at least he could prep the car.

Five minutes later the patrol car rounded the corner in front of the Ratford Center and poked down the two-lane industrial drive at ten miles per hour. Sheriff Dennis immediately recognized the location. He frantically punched the door window buttons and the cluster of buttons on the console in front of him to no avail. Shane selected "Music" from the program menu and scrolled through the list of songs until he found "Heat Wave" by Martha and the Vandellas. The infectious 1960's tune played through the car's speakers at modest volume. The Sheriff ran his forearm over the beads of sweat on his forehead.

"Very funny. I want you to talk to me. I want you to tell me why you're doing this."

The car slowly positioned itself in spot number #44 in the Ratford Building parking lot, where leftover bits of yellow police tape rested on the asphalt. The engine puttered as Sheriff Dennis waited for a response. By this time the heater fan had cut on and the temperature within the car had already risen to one hundred three degrees. It was 12:55 in the afternoon, just five minutes before the sunbeams would hit the mirrored building at the precise angle. Heat was already radiating off the dashboard in a wavy haze. The Sheriff's mouth was parched when he spoke out again.

"Please, tell me why you're doing this."

Shane positioned the microphone up to his mouth and clicked on "Morph" to disguise his voice. He chose "Adult Male" from the pull-down, then spoke.

"Grab the phone."

Sheriff Dennis hesitated for a moment, then reached over and withdrew the plastic bag containing Shane's phone from a box on the passenger seat. He carefully pulled the smartphone out and powered it on. A faint tone sounded, and a myriad of colored icons displayed atop a graphic of a blue minivan. Something about it already seemed familiar.

"Tap on Completed."

The Sheriff followed the command from the GPS voice. A grid of image thumbnails immediately displayed. He could tell before he clicked on any of them that they were photos of all the accident victims.

"I don't want to look at these," he responded. "Why did you do this to these people?"

There was a pause that seemed to last a full minute—and every second counted. The inside temperature had climbed to one hundred ten. Shane needed his phone back, so it must remain intact. On it was a beta version of the mobile app. He unchecked the morph algorithm and spoke in his own voice.

"Because they're bad drivers, Sheriff Dennis. They ran red lights. They tailgated. They cut people off. They were aggressive, and often rude. They put other people's lives in jeopardy. I'm doing what you do all day long: preventing innocent people from losing their lives because of the stupidity of others. I just make sure there are no repeat offenders.

It was true. Sheriff Dennis had developed a deep disdain for those who took to the roads and endangered other drivers and pedestrians alike. The ones who seemed to think it was their God-given right to drive however they pleased. He had seen way too many accidents, even before the recent surge.

"Remember when you said someone as young as me shouldn't be seeing accidents like the one on Calvert?" Shane continued.

Sheriff Dennis listened to the boy while examining other

folders on his smartphone. He called up pictures of the teen when he was just a toddler. A few showed him playing in the front yard with his baby sister. Others revealed him camping with his family, the blue minivan featured prominently in the background.

Then he clicked on the folder labeled, simply, "Mom." Several images of a beautiful woman with a captivating smile and caring eyes displayed. In one picture she had her arm draped over the shoulder of a younger Shane, who couldn't have been more than six years old at the time. It all flooded back to him. That day when he saw that same woman hunched over the steering wheel of her minivan, her gentle face battered and bloodied. And then watching the crew remove the door, hoping that she would be spared, too. And then seeing that her lower half had been separated from her upper half by a slab of steel from the other car. And all that darkened blood that puddled onto the car seat and dripped onto the floor.

And then there were the cries that haunted him every night since. The cries of a young boy who clung to his leg and pleaded for his *momma* to be okay. How he stood at the side of the road and rubbed that child's head with one hand and his own tears with the other. How he knelt down and turned the child into his chest so he wouldn't see his mother's corpse removed from the wreckage. And how the sobs that moistened his blue shirt faded into the painful pleas of an innocence forever marred.

"M*omma...momma...momma.*"

He rubbed his eyes of what moisture was left in him, and spoke.

"I know," he said, "I was there."

Shane remembered, too, at that moment. He remembered the kind man that took him back to the station and gave him a candy sucker. The man that wetted a rag and wiped away his tears while telling him to be strong for his little sister and his father. And how he looked him in the eye and said his mother would always be with him, because a mother never stops loving her child, even when they can't be together. And then there was the warmth of the man's embrace and the softness of his voice as he said this. Shane heard that same softness now.

"Then you know what we have to do. We need to work together. Are you with me?"

It was 1:02 p.m. and the car had reached one hundred fifteen degrees inside. The light glistened off the Ratford Building with a blinding white intensity, as if it were a message from a place far above.

"Yes, I'm with you, son," the Sheriff responded. "I want to know how you're able to control these cars like you do."

"Bring back my phone, and I'll show you." Shane tilted his tablet forward and the patrol car rolled away from the scorching parking spot. Then the windows unrolled, the seat belts loosened, and the heater switched over to a refreshing burst of cool air.

"She's all yours."

Sheriff Dennis promptly returned the phone to Shane at his home. With his family still away, Shane explained the inner workings of his program, which he called "Street Saver 2021." Less than a year ago he had taken apart one of the GPS tracking devices now required in all vehicles. Inside was a tiny chip, no bigger than a thumbnail, which didn't seem to have anything to do with the device's purpose. He broke apart trackers from other auto manufacturers' models and found identical chips. They all had the code "RM666" stamped on them. It became clear what they were doing once he hacked into the internal marketing and research department of one of those U.S. manufacturers.

"It was meant for more than finding a vehicle," Shane explained. "They wanted to know how often you drove your car, where you drove your car, and what businesses you visited. It could analyze that behavior and sell it to advertisers. They already let advertisers flash ads onto your GPS screen as you approach nearby stores."

But that wasn't all. He explained that the tiny chip was a leftover component from the failed self-driving-car craze, which became a cover for a covert National Security Agency initiative. It could interact with all the modules within the car's main computer—steering, braking, acceleration, locks, seat belts, windows, atmosphere control—to allow your car to be remotely commandeered for virtually any reason. After the secret program was scrapped, auto manufacturers intended to sell the control capability to advertisers. You could simply tell your GPS what you wanted to buy, and it would deliver you to the nearest place that offered it. And even if you weren't looking to buy anything, it could *steer* you in the direction of a purchase anyway.

"Why allow a driver to have free will to choose where they want to go when you can control that for them." Sheriff Dennis thought of the repercussions.

"But I knew there was a better purpose for all this technology." Shane called up the green grid. By hacking into the Department of Motor Vehicles, he was able to generate a database of all locally owned vehicles, including make, model, license plate number, and Vehicle Identification Number. When he cross-referenced that data with the hacked manufacturers' data, he was able to retrieve the unique remote codes required to operate any vehicle. The manufacturers had also developed a real-time map program, which included business locations, posted speed limits, traffic lights, and more. His program analyzed which vehicles were violating traffic laws and would automatically flag them. "See the cars flashing red? Those are the ones that just did something wrong. They are ready to be tagged."

Shane clicked on one of the red cars and a virtual version of it appeared on his tablet screen. "I turned those pictures I've been taking into 3D replicas. Would you like to have your hand at this one, Sheriff Dennis? The magnifying glass doesn't end until three o'clock."

Two weeks later the World Order Alliance approved Shane's application, and his video game went public. Public, rather, to the worldwide underground community of expert gamers who scored highest on other racing games. These were the best virtual drivers, less likely to cause accidents with non-offending vehicles. The WOA added the stipulation that once a bad driver was tagged, their hazard lights should flash as a warning for others to get out of the way.

Points were garnered for the number of completed tags in a given time, with added bonuses for the most macabre kills. Gamers were encouraged to take pictures of the dead drivers, which would later be incorporated into the game's visual effects. After all, what's the fun without a gruesome payoff?

Auto manufacturers remained silent about all the new accidents. They were ordered to, or their true intentions would be exposed to the public. And the Feds mysteriously dropped their investigation.

Sheriff Dennis got a cut of the game sales, including the mobile app that followed. But he also shared in the satisfaction that expert overseers were maintaining his streets. Who would have thought that in 2021, and beyond, the safety of the driving world would be in the hands of young video gamers?

The public was paranoid, as they should be. But driving considerably improved. Everyone knew that hazard lights meant certain death. Some reveled in seeing bad drivers caught. Others knew it was only a matter of time before they slipped up. Like Stanley Willis, who drove through a stop sign in Albuquerque, New Mexico, on March 3, 2022. In a live voice, Sheriff Dennis took to his microphone in the basement of his home and merrily ushered in the next victim.

"You've been tagged. Your virtual player is Fuzz4Justice from Lakeland, Florida. Good luck, and good riddance."

PEOPLE WHO NEED TO DIE

Cell Phonies

Jim and Tammy Philips were taking their vows on that warm June afternoon in Meadowbrook, Texas, when they looked out among their friends. Half of them were texting on their cell phones. Of the remaining half, half of those people were recording the event on their phones, their raised hands blocking the views of those who were actually "in attendance."

Sam Stevens sat at the Applebee's on Liberty Street in Madison, Wisconsin, after a long day working at Parker's Body Shop. What he craved most, other than the tall Miller Lite the bartender placed in front of him, was conversation. But of the five people who had arrived since he walked in, three were playing games on their smartphones, one was texting, and the fifth came in for carry-out.

Paula Townsend had just picked up her six-year-old son at Grover Elementary in Cedar Rapids, Iowa, when her cell phone rang. It was her friend from Yoga class who wanted to ask for a ride the following day. The second that Paula reached for her phone to answer her was the same second that nine-year-old Tim Seaver, and his little sister, four-year-old Amy Seaver, stepped onto Sycamore Street. Paula couldn't swerve in time.

Applications for eradicating distracted and distracting cell phone users flooded the government. Only three were approved.

ONE.

Former prison guard Josh McMillan had seen his share of suffering. Torture, fasting, and riots were all too common at the old Salisburg Correctional Facility in Pennsylvania. When it shut down in 1997 after the Devries scandal—one of the inmates, Jeffrey Devries, was found hanging in his cell with a remote control taped to his hand—Josh returned to school to pursue a degree in psychology. About that time, cell phones were becoming increasingly pervasive in the social landscape. Phone companies were merging into giant conglomerates, smaller phones were being manufactured, and people were "cutting the cord" that kept them tethered to their home phones. Ads for cell phones flooded the airways.

After receiving his Doctorate in Psychology in 2004, Josh spent three years working at a major phone carrier, using what he learned to lure aging holdouts into the cell phone market. The psychology behind the company's ads, which Josh helped create with the marketing director, was personal freedom—freedom to be in touch whenever you wanted and wherever you wanted. Narcissism and ego, combined with the gratification of acknowledgment, played heavily into the ad development. The ads were highly successful.

By 2010, cell phones had all but eradicated the landline market. Laws had been proposed to fine users for texting while driving, but cell phone company lobbyists made sure those laws were watered down, and states lacked the funding to enforce them.

In 2013, airlines proposed that cell phones could be used inflight, and although there was a huge backlash from those who opposed it, the airlines conceded to a generation who believed it was their own personal right to speak on their phones anywhere—even to the discomfort of others. Now if you wanted peace and quiet on a flight, you had to pay extra for a phone-free section.

Josh regretted having set this train in motion through his early years at the phone company. After a seven-year stint as a clinical psychologist in Boca Raton, Florida, he returned to Salisburg, Pennsylvania, in 2020 and became the director for the Salisburg Addiction Center. When the order came down, he knew what he had to do to set things straight.

Project Cellparation was the name of the experimental program that sought to break users of their cell phone addiction. Knowing that the most ardent cell phone users would never admit they had a problem, Josh employed cunning tactics to lure them in. "Be Smarter with your Smartphone," "101 Ways to Make Your Cell Phone Work For You," and "Your Phone, Your Friend," were just a few of the programs listed online incognito. There was no mention of an affiliation with an addiction center. Instead, it was presented as a three-day "exclusive" seminar to be held at the Salisburg Historical Manor, not more than half a mile from the abandoned Salisburg Correctional Facility.

News of the program, with promises of keynote speakers from major smartphone manufacturers like Apple and Samsung, attracted everyone from CEOs to soccer moms. In order to narrow enrollment down to one hundred, applicants were asked to fill out an online form that sought to undercover their level of usage. Those who checked "Over six hours a day" for how much time they spent using their phones, and also said they couldn't go a day without them, were given first preference. These were the users who needed "correcting" the most.

"Welcome to the Salisburg Historical Manor." Josh greeted the first arrivals on the morning of Day 1. The vacant ballroom of the manor was the setting for the initial orientation. "You'll find coffee and orange juice over by the far wall. Thank you for coming."

Before opening the doors, Josh had slipped scopolamine, also known as the "zombie" drug or "Devil's Breath," into the drinks to make the attendees more "compliant." He had read about it in a medical journal. Criminals used it in Colombia, where it is harvested from the Borrachero tree, to make victims willfully commit crimes, empty their bank accounts, and turn over their possessions. The drug, sometimes used for motion sickness, also blocks the acetylcholine receptor in the brain, which is responsible for retaining memory. Victims do what they're told, then forget what they've done. It was the perfect class supplement.

"Now that you are all here," Josh continued at 10 a.m., "I want everyone to introduce yourself to each other. Feel free to mingle for the next twenty minutes." By doing so, he was assured that everyone would ingest the drug. But he needed to know if it really worked.

"Okay, let's return to our seats. I will now begin your orientation. Everyone, please raise your hands while holding your smartphones."

Shiny glass screens reflected rays from the nearby window as all one hundred cell phone addicts simultaneously held up their devices. It was an odd sight, almost like a hail to Hitler.

"Okay, now I want you to turn them off."

"I'd like to record the seminar, if you don't mind." The request came from a heavyset man in a blue suit sitting near the middle of the room—one of those guys who acted like a big shot because he got lucky and scored a good job, but you could tell he was just a gold chain around his neck from selling used cars. Josh slowly walked over to the man.

"Now, how will you be able to pay attention to the class when you're worried about recording it correctly?"

"I just thought that," the man paused, "well, I guess you do have a point there." The drug was making its way through his bloodstream. "You're right, I don't know what I was thinking."

Precisely, Josh thought.

"Now that all of you have your smartphones off, it's time to place everyone into groups of four. These will be your make-believe *friends*. For the three days, your *friends* will help you understand your phones better. Group yourselves in the order you are seated. Count off four and get to know your *friends'* names."

The attendees turned forward and backward to greet one another. Out of instinct, some wanted to grab their smartphones and enter them as contacts. Josh witnessed one woman poking her hand as if an invisible keypad were there. Their dependence was worse than he thought.

"Okay, now that everyone has familiarized yourselves with your friends, we will begin our first exercise: Your Phone, Your Friend. You may now pick up your phone...then hand it to one of the friends in your group."

This small request proved to be a challenge for many of the attendees. Allowing someone else to touch his or her phone, let alone take possession of it, seemed akin to turning over a child. Even with the effect of the drug, some refused to do it at first. Josh reassured them that it would only be for a moment.

"Okay. Now, describe the phone's appearance in detail to its owner. Make it sound delicious. There *is* a point to all of this, no matter how silly it may seem at first. You can go ahead now."

Sleek, sensual, sexy, playful, functional were just a few of the adjectives used in the exercise. Some of the members gave the phones Vanna White up-and-down swooshes for accent. Many of the owners reached back for their phones, the separation from them too great. Josh observed the intense attachment of his captive subjects with their devices. It made him smile.

"You may now give the phones back to their rightful owners."

Heavy sighs resounded throughout the room as the exchange took place. "Oh, thank God!" one woman exclaimed.

"I can see that your phones mean a lot to all of you," Josh continued. "It is, indeed, your friend. But your friend is missing something that you have. A heartbeat. This next exercise is important. I want you to load up your phone's sound-recording app, and when I give you the call, place the phone close to your chest and record your heart beating for one full minute. Put it under your clothing so the audio will be clear."

Buttons unbuttoned and zippers unzipped as the drugged attendees followed the latest order.

"Okay, now that your apps are loaded and you are ready, let's have one minute of silence. When I say start, record your heartbeat."

Josh looked around the room. All the attendees had their eyes closed and fingers waiting to tap.

"Start."

It was an eerie silence. Josh slowly rocked back and forth in front of the room as he witnessed the obedience of the attendees. How powerful the scopolamine must be for complete strangers to partially undress and carry out his commands. If he could get them to do this, what more could he make them do over the next two days? The minute passed like an ode to someone's death.

"Okay, stop."

As if coming out of a hypnotic trance, all the attendees simultaneously opened their eyes and ended their recordings.

"Good. Very good." Josh sat down in his chair. "Okay, for the next hour I want you to put on your headphones and play back the recording of your own heartbeat. Listen to it as if it were the only sound in the world. Get to know the rhythm, how many beats it beats in a minute. I want it to be your new music. I want you to fully understand that your phone is more than a device that helps you throughout the day. Your phone is an extension of yourself."

The room of attendees reached for their earphones.

"When the hour is up," Josh continued, "you can return back

to your hotel rooms and do the same. Play with your phone; use every app. And as you go to sleep tonight, let the sound of your heartbeat fill the room. Put the recording on loop. I want this to be the sound that soothes you. There is a point to all this, you will see."

After the class dismissed, Josh walked through the woods behind the Salisburg Manor and exited onto Old Chapmore Road. Within a few minutes he was back at the abandoned Salisburg Correctional Facility where he would spend the night preparing.

Day 2 of the three-day seminar began with everyone meeting back at the Salisburg Manor ballroom. Before they entered, Josh had doubled the amount of scopolamine in the coffee and juices.

"You all look very rested. How did it go last night?"

"I used apps I hadn't touched in months," said one man. "I didn't know my phone could do so much."

"I loved falling asleep to the sound of my heartbeat," added a woman in the front of the room. The others nodded their heads in agreement.

"That's good. So you're beginning to understand how very, *very* important your phone is to you."

"Absolutely."

"Today we will move on to how effectively you use your phone to communicate with others. I want you to call every single one of your contacts and speak to them. Talk as long as you can hold them on the phone. The goal here is to always be in conversation with someone."

"Won't it get loud in here?" asked the same man who wanted to record the event on the first day. "It might be distracting."

"Indeed. It's a nice day out, so feel free to roam about the manor gardens as you place your calls. That will give you some space."

"But I just text people; I never talk on the phone," added a woman in the back of the room.

"For those of you who only text, raise your hands." About fifty percent of the class responded. "Okay, for you, I want you to text all your contacts. I want to see those fingers typing continuously. You can stay in the room here, if you so wish. You may begin when you're ready."

Half the class exited the main doors and moved about the manicured lawn. Some stood under trees as they placed their calls; others lost themselves within the maze of hedges and flower beds. The din of jabber scared away the birds and squirrels.

Inside, fingers tapped incessantly away at glass screens, filling the room with clicking sounds. It was as if a new species of insect had invaded the building. Electronic crickets.

Josh walked about the room and gardens, observing how elated the attendees seemed to get when contacting others. His early research revealed that receiving texts and talking sent packets of dopamine into the bloodstream. Combined with the scopolamine, this put the attendees into a frenzied high. After each call, outside attendees frantically dialed another number to get another fix. He had observed this pattern for decades in the real world: a driver holding up his or her phone after a call was over to see whom else they could contact. The immediacy of the gratification was addicting.

It wasn't until 1 p.m. that Josh called the attendees back into the building. When they were seated he made an eyebrow-raising request: "Turn over your phones."

"Just for lunch," he added, which lessened the stir. "Place your phones into this basket up front, and I'll see you back here at 2 p.m. You'll find several eateries down the street."

The drugged attendees obediently beelined for the restaurants. Doubling the scopolamine had a peculiar effect: it made them both compliant and obsessive at the same time. Josh took note of this. Once alone, he systematically attached each of the phones to his tablet by an ultra-USB cable. An impish grin crossed over his face as he extracted the necessary data.

"Tomorrow," Josh said to the returning attendees as he handed back their phones, "we'll be going on a little field trip. Make sure you get plenty of rest."

"Is that when we get to meet the guest speakers?"

"Yes, you'll all have some one-on-one time with top experts. But tomorrow will really test how important your phone is to you. So, again, I want you to take your phones home and listen to your heartbeat recording as you sleep. Turn the volume up so it permeates your dreams."

Josh neglected to tell the attendees that he had installed an app on each of their phones intended to super-addict them to their devices through hypnosis. The recording that would play in the backdrop of their heartbeats was simple, but undetectable to the conscious ear: "Your phone is your soul. Your phone is your soul."

"We will meet back here in the morning, and go from there."

The evening air was thick and damp as Josh maneuvered through the woods back to the Salisbury Correctional Facility. All the necessary preparations would be completed on this night. As he walked along the dingy corridors of empty cells—paint peeling off the walls and bars sheathed in rust—he ruminated over his days as a prison guard there. He remembered how some inmates received "special" treatment for their disobedience. It always fascinated him how far the human spirit could be pushed before it snapped. The Jeffrey Devries experiment was his proudest accomplishment.

These people were no different, he thought. Distracted and distracting cell phone users were just as much a menace as thieves and murderers. Their actions ultimately fray the fabric of society. Some end up taking innocent lives through their intentional disregard. He couldn't wait to see them suffer.

On Day 3, Josh tripled the dose of scopolamine, even sprinkling a powdered form of the drug on top of the doughnuts he had purchased. Attendees were directed to "eat and drink up" as they entered the ballroom for a final time. "You'll need the energy," Josh added.

Afterward, the fully compliant attendees snaked through the woods behind the manor with no sense of how peculiar it was to be led to an abandoned prison. Some seemed inspired by the inventiveness of it all. Upon entering the main prison doors, Josh commanded them to turn over their phones to him again. He then directed the hundred attendees to divide themselves up into their original groups of four.

"Your cell friends are now your cell mates," Josh said with a smile as his followers reached the inner corridors. "These will be your holding cells for the duration of your test. As you can see, each cell is equipped with a large water jug. Drink as much as you need." The water had also been spiked with scopolamine the night before.

His victims willingly entered each of the twenty-five prison cells. After Josh locked each cell door, he left the cell block for several minutes. When he returned, he stood in the central open area with a view to everyone.

"Today will test your loyalty to your cell phones. I can see right now that some of you are having a hard time without your phones in your possession." A few of the victims had their faces pressed up to the bars like puppies in a dog pound. Josh pulled a cell phone out of his pocket and held it up for everyone to see.

"Like, I wonder who owns this one?"

Shards of glass and plastic scattered for several yards as the phone abruptly smashed to the floor. A thunderous gasp rippled down the cell block.

"Obey my every word today, and this will not happen to yours."

Josh walked back up to the first corridor. "I will now release

38

the first five cells. You will follow me through the metal doors and down the north corridor to several rooms. It is in those rooms that you will be tested."

By now the drug had completely subdued the fight-or-flight response of Josh's captive subjects. The first twenty followed him like lemmings to a sea cliff. It was an eerie sight along the way, like something out of a *Ghost Hunters* episode. The walls were gray with chipped paint and the occasional graffiti. Dimly lit rooms with metal tables, bedpans, and rusty fixtures made it seem more like an abandoned hospital than a prison. There was a heavy stench of aged piss and mildew. Eventually, they reached the woodworking workshop once used for prisoner rehabilitation.

"I want ten of you to take a seat in the chairs I have provided; the rest of you can stand by. In front of each chair is a box constructed out of six one-foot-square pieces of plywood. The base of the box has two hinged flaps that form a circle in the center when folded up, just large enough to surround an average neck. You will also see that the flaps can be locked into place. The boxes are equipped with inward-facing speakers on both sides, which will be wirelessly connected to a playback console on my tablet. I call them chatterboxes."

The victims seemed fascinated by this peculiar experiment.

"In this test you will listen to your phone conversations, which I recorded and downloaded from your phones yesterday, and analyze how well you communicate with others. If you texted, you will hear someone else's conversations. In any event, you are to position the boxes over your heads, and I will lock them into place. This will provide you with the required solitude." He smiled as the group followed his orders.

Josh walked around the ten subjects and secured the wood flaps up around their necks, then closed the padlocks to prevent the boxes from being removed. Then he walked over to his tablet and started the recordings.

"Okay, I will be back to check on you in an hour or so. The

rest of you follow me."

Josh directed five of the remaining ten subjects to enter the room two rooms down, then sent the other five into an adjacent room and locked the door. In the first room he had the subjects circle around a metal table on which sat five cylindrical vats filled with a clear liquid. At the bottom of the vats were phones encased in clear boxes.

"Your phone is important to you, yes?"

The subjects nodded in unison.

"I have separated your own phones from the basket and placed them inside the vats you see in front of you. Don't worry, they are safe."

"That's mine!" one of the victims pointed out.

"Go ahead and stand in front of the vat that contains your phone," Josh directed.

The group shuffled around the table.

"How important is your phone to you?"

"*Very* important," one man responded while drooling over his iPhone 10c.

"Good. Then all you have to do is reach into the vat and pull out the clear box that holds it. Would anyone like to try?"

"I will!" shouted the same man.

"Go ahead."

The others watched as the man pulled up his sleeve and immediately thrust his arm into the two-foot-high cylinder in front of him. Effervescent bubbles quickly formed on his skin, which peeled off his arm in large chunks. Within seconds the clear liquid turned red. A horrendous grimace shot over his face as he pulled out the flesh-stripped bones where his arm once was. Moments later he fell to the floor.

"This is the acid test," Josh said without hesitation. "There is, however, one vat that contains mere water. So maybe one of you will be lucky enough to retrieve your phone unscathed."

The remaining four seemed more intent on getting their

phones back than on the dying man beside them.

"Oh, and don't think that you can dab a piece of your clothing or something else into the vat to check. The acid in these vats only eats away at skin. I will leave you now and check back in an hour. Again, how important is your phone to you?"

Josh locked the door behind him and proceeded to the next room where the remaining five victims were waiting. On one side of the room, five metal chairs with leather straps attached to them were welded to each other arm-to-arm. On the other side of the room, the front end of a 1966 Plymouth Fury jutted out of the wall like something you'd see at a car-themed restaurant. In between the chairs and the car front was a track and pulley system.

"Let me start by saying that each of you will be receiving your phones back. That's because, in this experiment, you will be tested on your texting skills."

Josh commanded the subjects to sit in the chairs. He tightly fastened the leather straps around their ankles, forearms, necks, and chests. Their hands had about a six-inch range of motion in front of them, just enough to hold on to their phones. Josh returned the phones to each user.

"You've heard of texting while driving. In this experiment you'll be texting while *surviving*. Above the car in front of you is a large screen. Random texts will flash across it momentarily. You must retype those texts on your cell phones exactly as you see them, without making any mistakes. If you make mistakes, or fail to keep up, the electronically controlled cables at your feet will incrementally pull all your chairs toward the car front some twenty feet away."

"How long do we have to text?" asked the woman in the center seat.

"Until you no longer see texts on the screen." Josh grabbed another tablet and started the experiment. The first text across the screen read: "Texting while driving increases your chance of an accident twenty-three fold."

"You may begin. I will check back with you soon."

While Josh set up the first three experiments, the other eighty attendees became antsy in their cells, like feral cats. Many drank the supplied water, ingesting more scopolamine in the process. Their faces reddened as they paced back and forth.

Josh reentered the chatterbox experiment room and upped the volume of the recorded phone conversations. A few of the subjects jolted out of their seats. Ten minutes later, Josh superimposed several recorded conversations on top of each other, then increased the volume again. This immediately sent the captive subjects circling around the room. Some grasped at the sides of the wooden boxes and attempted to pull them off. This was Josh's cue.

"We are now entering the second phase of this experiment," he said over a microphone and into their speakers. "You can hear several loud conversations going on at once. Distracting, yes? It's not too pleasant, is it?"

Josh torqued the volume up a notch.

"I want you to know what it's like being out in public with people just like you, who can't seem to stop talking on their fucking phones while around others. I guess you feel empowered doing so, almost like you're entitled to disrupt the peacefulness of the world."

Josh increased the volume a bit more.

"For over thirty years we've had to deal with you—in the subways, in the grocery stores, in the lines at the Post Office, at the airports, in restaurants, in our parks, and just about every space you can invade. You forgot, or maybe you never knew, that conversations with others aren't supposed to be broadcast to the people around you. It's not fair to them, and it's not fair to the person you have on the other end."

Josh walked around to each of the subjects and placed a single tool from a toolbox into their hands, which they blindly accepted. He returned to the microphone.

"There's only one way out for you. Luckily, you have a choice, unlike the many people you've disturbed over the years."

On that, Josh cranked the volume to full and left the room.

Chaos ensued as the ten victims struggled to free themselves from the confines of the chatterboxes. One man took the hatchet in his hand and beat the sides of the box, slowly at first, then with full force in large swings. The final blow split the side and lodged the hatchet deep into his skull. A woman drilled directly into her neck while attempting to dislodge the locking mechanism on the box's underside. Another man frantically sawed through the front and into his forehead. Others beat their heads repeatedly against the cinder block walls to no avail. Their demise was more maddening. Mental trauma.

In the acid room, three more of the five subjects had lost their limbs, and their lives. Josh entered the room just as the remaining woman was about to retrieve her phone.

"Wait!" Josh commanded. The woman looked up. "How do you know that's actually water in there?"

"Because you told us one was safe?"

"Why would you believe me? After all, look at your colleagues. They're all dead."

At that precise moment, the phone inside the cylinder flashed an incoming message.

"Well," Josh continued, "it looks like someone is contacting you." The message read, "What's up, Nicole?"

"This is your chance, Nicole. This is your decisive moment. Is it really worth answering that message? On the other hand, perhaps you can text back and get the police here. Then you can be free." Josh walked toward the door. "I'll leave you to decide."

Sweat ran down the woman's forehead. Her heart raced. "Let's get together this week" popped up in another message balloon. She attempted to tip over the vat, but it was bolted to the metal table. Nothing in the room presented itself as a tool to reach inside, though the thought of using one of the good arms from a corpse crossed her mind. "Are you there?" was the message that finally sent her own arm down inside the cylinder.

As she fumbled with the clear case that housed her phone, the liquid surrounding her arm began to gel. Then it quickly solidified, locking her in place. The quick-drying epoxy had interacted with the moisture in her skin, causing a chemical reaction that altered its state. "I guess I'll let you go" was the ironic final message that popped up on the screen. Her phone obsession had literally sealed her fate.

Back in the texting room, the five victims frantically poked away at their screen keyboards. Their fingers blistered while attempting to mimic line after line of inane messages displaying in front of them. The chairs had already moved three feet forward.

"I can't do this anymore!" yelled one of the subjects.

"You have to or we'll be crushed into the grille of that car!" shouted another.

Josh stood in the back of the room for a moment, then walked up to the chairs and leaned his head into the ear of the man on the right.

"How does it feel to know that what you do to risk so many lives, texting, is now the only thing that will save yours?"

The line of chairs inched ahead as the man fell behind in his typing. Josh circled around to the other side where a woman furiously tapped away. "Typos will cost you," he gleamed, before moving to the side of the car front.

"The texts you see on the screen right now are the final conversations of those who died in car accidents while texting, or caused the deaths of others by their negligence. I want you to remember these when you meet your own fate today."

Josh was about to leave the room when one of the victims

accidentally dropped her phone. The cable system immediately engaged and sent the five forward like dummies in a crash simulator. Blood splattered for several yards when the chairs collided with the car grille. Chests crushed under impact. One victim's head was impaled by the car's hood ornament. The man on the right was barely alive when Josh walked over to inspect his work.

"You know, when I'm driving in my car, and I see other people texting in theirs and driving erratically, putting everyone around them in danger, including me, I will remember this moment." Josh pulled the man's head back by his hair as he breathed a final gasp. "Your minutes are up."

Overdoses of scopolamine had increased the anxiety levels of the remaining attendees. Some appeared almost rabid. Josh took advantage of the drug-induced paranoia before releasing another twenty victims for his next experiment.

"Only one of you in each remaining cell will get your phone back," he said before leading the others away. "Take a look around at your friends, your cell mates. Do you trust them? Remember, they took your phone away from you on the first day."

Josh guided the new group beyond the three experiment rooms and into a large, darkened room illuminated by tiny pinhole lights. A rhythm of low-level heartbeats rippled through the air like a sacrificial ritual in a movie.

"In this room are all your phones. The dots you see are the battery lights. The sounds you hear are your own heartbeats. After I blindfold you, you will have twenty minutes to find your phone. If you don't all have your own phones in your hands within that time, you will die."

Josh wrapped thick duct tape around each of their heads before leaving and locking the doors.

The phone volumes incrementally increased as the minutes

passed. Frantic movements led to bodies colliding and limbs twisting in unnatural ways.

"Be quiet, I need to hear my heartbeat!" shouted one victim.

Ten minutes in, the sound was deafening, like a large stethoscope over a thousand wombs. In their scopolamine dazes, many of the victims fell to the floor and aimlessly crawled about. The first two to reach a phone were met with sharp rebar rods through their chests. One man found his phone instantly, but was shocked to death by the attached live wire. Others succumbed to open pits in the floor and more carefully placed booby-traps.

After the twenty minutes had elapsed, a timer on one of the phones triggered large amounts of carbon monoxide into the air. The remaining captives stumbled around the room, wavered, then collapsed. Now they could only drag themselves around in the darkness. Within minutes the only heartbeats left were those from the recordings. It was like Poe's "Tell-Tale Heart."

Agonizing screams and moans from death throes echoed throughout the corridors while Josh disposed of the bodies in the first four experiments. He returned to the holding cells to witness the gruesome aftermath of scopolamine intoxication. There were mangled corpses and bodies with limbs askew barely holding on to life. In a couple of cells, split-open heads stuck to the vertical bars like large insects splayed over car radiator fins. Survivors cowered in the corners, lapping up spilled droplets of spiked water.

"I see you've done my work for me," Josh said as he paced along the cell block with his arms behind his back. "You've seen that your cell mates couldn't be trusted, and you took appropriate action."

Josh took inventory. Of the remaining fifteen cells, only twelve had a lone survivor. Forty-eight subjects had succumbed to the scopolamine frenzy.

"*Perfect*," Josh whispered. "As promised, the victors will get their smartphones back." Upon hearing this, the twelve men and women pressed their heads up to the bars and stretched their arms through like animals in a zoo. "You will be my twelve disciples, and I will lead you to salvation. For you now know that your smartphone *is* your salvation. It is your *soul*. Without it, you would perish."

Josh paused in front of Cell #73. It had been twenty-four years since he stood there eyeing Jeffrey Devries' lifeless body. Back then the addiction was television, and a handful of guards took sadistic pleasure in torturing prisoners who couldn't seem to live without it. They made Devries' death look like a hanging: twisting his bed sheet into a tight rope, looping it around his neck, and dangling him from the overhead support beam. But he was dead well before they placed him back into his cell.

It was easier than he thought, leading his disciples to the far north end of the building to the twelve death-row cells. Some held hands as if they were in second grade and heading down a school hallway. Josh coaxed them along, telling them that each had passed the seminar "with flying colors." None of the survivors were aware of what happened to their colleagues.

In each cell was a small wooden chair. Josh strapped the subjects down to it with duct tape. He taped their phones between their bound hands so only their thumbs could access the features.

"It is with great pleasure that I reward you for your tenacity. You all look a little peaked, so I'm going to attach an IV to you to make you feel better. I apologize for making you wait so long." In each cell, Josh pulled up a small plastic tube that ran outside of the cell and connected with a T-shaped connector to a longer tube. He attached a needle to the free end in his hand and jabbed it directly into the arm of each subject. None of them paid much attention, their focus now on starting up their phones and checking their messages.

"I apologize for the terrible reception in here. No bars when you're behind bars, I guess. But perhaps you can play some of your favorite games for a while, like you did on the first night."

Josh reached for his tablet and punched in a few numbers. He returned to each open cell and affectionately caressed the heads of the final victims as they tended to their phones.

At the end of the row, light from a small window glistened off the clear pouch of sodium pentothal as it slowly depleted over the next few hours. Like the Devries experiment, where use of the TV remote triggered a pump to push out the lethal drug, so did the smartphone activity—

Tap by tap, drip by drip.

TWO.

Ju Huang was only fourteen when she developed the SmoGo app in her small town of Taihu near Beijing, China. The program, which garnered over seventy million downloads in its first year, pinpointed precise locations in the country where smog levels were safe for outdoor activities. Meters attached to roaming messenger phones measured the amount of toxic particulates in the air. The retrieved data was extrapolated into a color-coded street map.

Air pollution had become a substantial problem in China with the surge of U.S. car imports over the previous decade. Even worse was the proliferation of smartphones. On average, every citizen of China had two phones at their disposal. Ju knew there was a need to eradicate excessive cell phone usage if her country was to socially prosper—and the best way to attack the problem was at the source.

With the SmoGo 2.1 update, every phone that downloaded the app also became a carrier of the Scarechi Trojan. The virus, which she also developed on her own, examined a user's likes and dislikes through social media, emails, and browser searches. It targeted their vulnerabilities and, at undisclosed times, made itself known in the form of loud and often obnoxious verbal and visual notifications. Basically, it would scare the shit out of people. Sometimes worse.

Lok Hu was traveling to work at the Qing Plastics plant when he noticed his car was low on gas. He pulled into a station for a fill-up. Today was a day he didn't want to be late, as rumors of a twenty-percent layoff had been circling throughout his department for weeks. He and his wife, Lei Hu, had just had their second child, and Lei stopped working to raise it.

It was a daily routine for Lok to commiserate with other employees through private emails. He also performed Google searches on Qing to see if any of the CEOs gave hint of what was to come. Many times he did so while driving. Lok left the gas station and returned to the busy highway.

The Scarechi app had an insidious side to it. It knew, through advanced GPS tracking, whether or not a person was driving, how fast they were driving, and the traffic patterns around them at any given time. It would strike at its most opportune moment.

"You will lose your job today," Scarechi chimed just as Lok was switching lanes to avoid a speeding car on his tail end. "You will lose your job today!" Scarechi shouted again in a dark, sinister tone.

Caught off guard, Lok swerved into the middle lane of the six lanes of heavy traffic at the same time that an eighteen-wheeler semi was doing the same. Seconds later, the front of Lok's car slid under the back of the trailer truck, crushing the roof on top of him and sending slabs of twisted metal deep into his body. The impact forced his head through the opening in the steering wheel, which crunched around his neck like a noose. In his final moments his eyes looked upon the screen of his phone, which rested on the floor just a foot away.

"One less driver, one less phone." Scarechi flashed a green smiley face, then turned the phone off.

Aashi Sarin from India was visiting China when her phone contracted the Scarechi virus from a colleague's email. On her twentieth birthday, her friend Baka took her to see *The Grudge 8* back home. Normally she never scared from these type of movies. Paranormal happenings, vampires, zombies, possessed demon children—all had become derivative. But she went along anyway.

Afterward, night after night, her phone would cut on while she lay sleeping. Eerie music from one of the scenes in the movie would play for several minutes, then stop. It was just low enough not to wake her, but enough to disrupt her conscious thoughts throughout the day.

Scarechi had noted what movie she watched because Aashi had texted several times in the theater. It was a bad habit of hers, one that upset many moviegoers, including her friend Baka. The virus also noted the death of Aashi's younger sister, Nileen, when Aashi sent text messages to her mother on the anniversary day.

Weeks later, the nighttime serenade triggered recurring dreams of Nileen's accident. The tragedy occurred on a warm May evening in 2017, just a week after Nileen's fifth birthday. The two were walking along the foot-high cement embankment that outlined the gorge in Malshej Ghat when Nileen slipped from her sister's hand. She tumbled down the 120-foot rocky gorge, dying instantly. Aashi still hadn't forgiven herself.

Months after returning from China, Aashi seemed to be in some sort of hypnotic trance every time the sinister music played at night. The dreams became increasingly disturbing. In them, her little sister beckoned her to return to the Malshej Ghat gorge to join her. And that's what she did.

On October 15, 2021, Aashi found herself at the exact spot where she lost her sister. Scarechi noted the coordinates and began the eerie music again, softly at first.

"This is where you killed me," a child's voice broke in before returning to the music at full volume. "You know what you need to do."

An hour later a tourist discovered Aashi's abandoned phone on the ledge and walked away with it.

Eventually, Scarechi had infected nearly half of the world's cell phones. Paul Lambert from Boise, Idaho, had a heart attack when his dead wife's face flashed onto the screen the day he tried to join a matchmaker group. Jill Vanhusen from London, England, stabbed her husband to death because she thought he was cheating on her. It only took one Internet search on infidelity for Scarechi to learn of her fears, then turn them against her in the form of random text messages from non-existent women. And Padre Esponza from Bogota, Colombia, got the shock of his life when Scarechi noted his illegal drug dealings and led the police directly to his front door. "That's a wr*app*!" was the final message on his confiscated phone. "Your friend, Scarechi. ;-)"

THREE.

At first it felt like a large candy bar, but only for a second. That's what Timothy Cook told himself when he fell victim to one of the Shovers on the streets of Peoria, Illinois. *Just think of it as a large candy bar, eaten at once.* Moments later he was gagging down the Samsung 7G cell phone he had just purchased a week prior. Once the phone lodged inside his throat, no amount of muscle contracting or grasping at his neck could loosen it free. A minute later he fell to the ground, his mouth agape, his eyes rolled upward.

Derrick Dixon was eighteen when a distracted cell phone driver killed his parents. The couple had just left their twentieth wedding anniversary dinner in downtown Pittsburgh when a man clipped them off on West Fulcrum Avenue. Their car crashed into a street lamp and sent both of them through the windshield.

The man was never convicted, though witnesses recalled seeing the phone up to his ear just before impact. Derrick vowed never to use a cell phone outside of his house again, and he would make sure others followed suit.

When the order came down, Derrick was already in trouble for spray-painting cryptic messages onto buildings and cars with his gang of followers. The Jerbs, as they called themselves, were once a strong force in many major U.S. cities. Initially, the gang of several thousand men was notorious for drug trafficking. But the worldwide legalization of marijuana took away much of their profit incentive. Addicts found marijuana a safer and more affordable alternative for a fix than heroin, meth, and other less-available substances.

Derrick rounded up his local posse of men on September 14, 2021 to make an announcement.

"We now have a means to make millions, more than on any drug we've sold on the streets. As you know, cell phone addiction is rampant. The World Order Alliance has given us the okay to take matters into our own hands. We will receive $100 for every cell phone user we remove from the streets. And there's plenty of them out there."

"How do we go about it?" asked one of the men.

"The key is we need to take them down with their cell phones so there is proof, before we get paid. My plan is simple."

And it *was* simple, almost ingenious.

Derrick and his vigilantes didn't concoct an elaborate ruse for luring cell phone addicts into fake seminars, nor design complex apps to destroy users surreptitiously. Their method was "shoving," and within weeks "The Shovers" would be feared worldwide.

Kelly Albright exited from the salon where she just received her third nail polishing in a month. She liked to splurge whenever she could, including on her pink, diamond-studded smartphone case. Others would ask where she got it and how much it cost.

"Oh, just $700," she'd say. "It makes me feel pretty inside."

The Dallas Shovers were pinged of her cell activity by a tower on top of the old Tallworth building a mile away. Cell phone towers had always been used to direct calls and data, but the World Order Alliance allowed an exclusive stream of GPS data to feed into the Shover's location app. With the app, Shovers were instantly alerted of excessive cell phone activity in the area. Within seconds they were upon her.

"Ma'am, you will need to hand us your phone," shouted a Shover sporting a "Down it Goes!" T-shirt.

The woman screamed and tried to run, but not before another Shover grabbed hold of her long blonde locks and pulled her to the ground.

"Your phone, now!"

Kelly reluctantly loosened her grip while the second Shover lowered himself to his knees. He positioned her head between his thighs and tilted it upward toward the sky. With his thumbs wrapped around her chin, he slowly pried her mouth open.

"Now, open wide. You know the drill," he taunted. The other Shover dialed the remover hotline with her phone, which tracked victims, before carefully inserting the phone into her mouth.

"Take it in, easy now. By the looks of you, this shouldn't be much of a stretch."

The sharp edges of the diamond inlays scraped over Kelly's tongue like a slow-moving cheese grater. Her eyes watered before closing tightly, as if doing so would remove her from the situation.

"That's right, all the way in."

Her legs and arms flailed when the phone reached the back of her throat. The two Shovers held her down: the first clamping his bended thighs tightly around her head, the other resting his full weight on her lower half.

With a quick jab of two fingers, the phone disappeared out of view. The skin in Kelly's neck pushed out a rectangular shape like an Adam's apple. Her breathless wheezing turned to silence in less than a minute.

The first Shover placed his hand on the mound as if checking her pulse. He waited for the phone to vibrate, a sign that the victim had been credited to their account. The WOA recorded the precise GPS location for coroner pickup while doing so.

"No early termination fees," the other Shover mocked.

The Shover community grew exponentially. It was easy money, and vigilantes were proud of the various techniques they used to track their victims. Others took great pleasure in luring their enemies into Shover GPS traps. There was a Shover newsletter, a Facebook page, Twitter account, and a reality TV show highlighting the most successful Shover gangs. It was even made into the number-one best-selling video game of 2021: "Grand Shovers."

Outdoor cell phone usage became a rarity. A person with a cell phone in their hand in public, whether they were talking on it or not, was considered a pariah. By the end of 2022, nearly four hundred million deaths were attributed to Shover activity, the Scarechi virus, and Josh's monthly seminars.

People mingled and talked directly to each other. Some just sat quietly and read a book, or contemplated about life. It was miraculous, to say the least, how well the world recovered from a technological addiction that threatened to destroy everything good about humanity.

Spammers

Six seconds was all it took. Less than the time to remove her shoes and place her keys into the basket by the door. Less than the time to pull back the bed covers and fluff up her pillow. Less than the time to say her prayers.

Laura Reed draped her long beige work coat over the back of the La-Z-Boy Imperial Walnut recliner she had purchased at the Sears closeout sale less than a year ago. She had saved fifty dollars on the chair, enough to purchase the decorative mosaic end table that sat next to it. Most all of the furnishings in her home were the result of discount sales and flea market finds. You wouldn't know it, though. Laura had impeccable taste. Everything went together beautifully, and she took great pride in creating a safe and peaceful place to live on a receptionist's budget.

After pouring a cup of lavender tea and changing into her comfortable jeans—Levi's 525s on sale half price—she sat in the recliner with her laptop and leaned back to lift the leg rest. Today had been an especially busy day. Her bosses at the law firm Markus, Wederman, and Feinstein, LLP, hadn't hired a replacement assistant after the blonde girl with the Marcia Brady smile returned to ASU for fall semester. This meant she had to come in an hour early each day to prepare the latest case files.

She didn't complain, though. She knew the rewards of a hard day's work, and sixteen years at the company had built her an impressive nest egg. Being thrifty also helped.

On this particular night, September 3, 2021, she spent an hour before dinner answering emails and reading her friends' social-media posts. Afterward, she laughed out loud during a rerun of *Will & Grace*, the one where Grace's water bra springs a leak at an art gallery. As the program ended, an email popped up on her laptop screen. It was from her bank. The subject: Your Deposit Summary.

During her lunch hour she had opened a savings account at Washama Bank, one of the largest banks in Arizona. They were the only bank left that offered free checking without a minimum balance. She transferred all her money to the account and deposited half of her bi-weekly check. The gentleman at the counter was very helpful, even providing her with pamphlets on their IRA accounts. At age 36, she needed to begin planning for her financial future.

It was nice to be able to access her account online, unlike the smaller bank she transferred from. Still, she was leery of scammers that filled her Inbox with junk mail every day. But this email seemed legit. It had the Washama logo—the silhouette of a bull inside a circle—and while hovering her cursor over "Click here to access your account balance," the link showed up in the lower portion of her browser as washama-online.com. She tapped the link and up popped a page with the same logo and a password/username form. After entering the two, it prompted her for the safeguard question: What is your dog's name? Though she didn't own a pet now, Sheba was the name she chose after the dachshund her parents gave her on her tenth birthday. Sheba lived to be fourteen years old, and Laura kept a picture of the beloved dog in her living room bookcase.

A tap on the Submit button sent her information across the Internet, leaving a spinning circle with the words "Accessing

Your Account...Please Wait" in place of it. Six seconds later the screen went blank. Laura waited a bit longer, then assumed the lack of response was due to Internet traffic. So she prepared for bed, turned off the lights, pulled the covers up tight around her shoulders, and contemplated what she might do over the weekend.

Six seconds was all it took. Six seconds for sixteen years of savings, $48,175.28, to be transferred to a bank in Nigeria and into the hands of twenty-two-year-old Onyango Ohingo.

It had been going on for two months now. John Fuller sent messages to Rachel at least three times a day. And she always responded, ending each one with a pink heart icon next to her name. He had resisted online dating sites for years after his nine-year marriage to Jennifer ended not at all harmoniously. But with the coaxing of his friends at the ad agency he worked at, he filled out a profile on MatchnMeet and was soon exchanging emails and messages with several women. Rachel stood out among the others: they both grew up in the same area of Indiana, they liked the same kinds of movies—edgy, thought-provoking films with no more than three characters—and she had a way of making him feel as though she really cared how his day went. She was a very attractive woman with a down-home charm that was hard to find in his cutthroat line of work.

It was time to pop the question.

Not, *do you want to get married*, of course, but do you want to talk on the phone and maybe meet on my next trip up north.

John carefully crafted his email.

Rachel, I always enjoy our online chats at night. I'll be in Chicago from August 24-26. It would be so nice to finally meet you. There's a coffee shop on Lake Shore Drive near Hyde Park. If you want, we can spend Saturday together, then hit up some of the restaurants and clubs at night. I hope you don't think it too forward, so let's talk on the phone. Truly mad about you, J.

He sent the message on a Friday and checked his mailbox every hour thereafter. Nothing. The following week the only emails that flipped up the red handle on his Inbox were work-related. He went on the trip alone and spent his off time in the hotel watching '90s sitcom reruns.

Indeed, Rachel had responded, within an hour after receiving his message. But the overzealous SPAM filters from John's email provider mistakenly flagged her email and sent it to his SPAM folder. Her reply:

Yes, John! I'd like that very much. My phone is 571-555-1297. I can't wait to hear your voice. Rachel ♥

Three months after his trip, John discovered Rachel's response while transferring files to a new computer. He immediately replied, but the email bounced back. The phone number had also been changed. He checked back on MatchnMeet where she had updated her profile to reveal her new status: In a relationship.

It was an unusually warm February, even in Arizona, when Laura and John met by happenstance at Martha's Cafe in downtown Phoenix. Laura had spent weeks trying to recover her lost funds, but even with the help of her law firm and bank, her search led to a dead end. Once the transfer was made, Onyango withdrew the money and closed his account.

"What's that you've purchased?" John looked over the top of his laptop while sipping an iced latte.

"One of those chocolate-filled danishes. They have the best baked goods here," Laura responded.

"I'll have to try it." John's computer blipped in a new email. "Just a second. I've won $500 in Cash! Sure I did. Delete."

"Better be careful, I had my life savings stolen from an email."

"You're kidding?"

"It happened in September. I clicked on a link in an email that I thought was from my bank. Once I entered my login information, my money was gone the next day. I found out when I tried to purchase a new dress."

"Didn't you think it was suspicious, the email, that is?"

"Well, I just opened an account that afternoon. I don't know how they could have linked my bank to my email and that I had just made a deposit."

"I've been doing some research on online scamming techniques. Was it a Friday that you received the email? They probably guessed that someone would be cashing their work check on a Friday, and impersonated the largest bank in the area. That would probably match a lot of people. I'm sorry to hear that that happened to you."

"I would *so* like to get back at these people."

"You and me both. I had a relationship cut short by SPAM. It wasn't something I clicked, though. I was tired of getting SPAM every day, and so I set my mail preferences to Medium to catch most incoming mail. Turns out that it can often flag legitimate email, like from the woman I was about to meet for a date. Ever since I missed her email, I keep my SPAM filter off. Now it's back to deleting one after another."

Blip.

"Do I want to try a free trial of Vydox today? No, thank you. Delete."

Laura smiled back. John continued.

"I don't even know what Vydox does. You'd think that after all these years they would have found a way to cut out spamming completely. I guess that's what we get for giving out our email addresses on all the sites we sign in to."

"We should have a big spammer convention and kill them

off."

"That would be something, ha ha." John looked back at Laura, who was delicately wiping her mouth with a napkin. She had a twinkle in her eye, as if the wheels were already spinning. Maybe she was serious. After all, she did lose all her money.

"We could be the Bonnie and Clyde of the Internet. Round up those thieves like cattle." The words coming out of her mouth even surprised Laura.

John closed his laptop and took a sip of coffee. "My name is John. I'm in."

"Laura. Laura Reed. It's nice to meet you, John."

The following weekend, John met Laura back at the same cafe. She opened up her laptop and started an Excel spreadsheet. John perused saved SPAM emails and read off the IP addresses from the header section of each message. These would help pinpoint which country and city the email was sent from. In the past, spammers would install malware on computers worldwide to mask the original sending address. Those computers were turned into "zombie" machines and would send out the SPAM for them. But with upgraded operating systems and improvements in virus protection, that was no longer possible.

"There's one problem." John spoke up a few minutes in. "Many of these IP addresses probably come from Internet cafes around the world. That's what they do. They log in under someone else's wi-fi so not to leave a trace."

Laura looked around at the nearby tables and alcoves where at least five other patrons were frantically typing away on their devices. "So there could be spammers in here right now?"

"Possibly. But most come from countries like Africa, China, and India. But there are still many in the U.S."

"So why don't we just reply to all the emails? Say something like, we are interested in learning more. Then mark the ones who respond."

"Good thinking. We can set up a fake email account and website for the 2022 Spammer Convention to be held in, say, Las Vegas, Nevada."

"Lure them in. Promise rewards. Say they're being rewarded for being effective spammers. Cash prizes and such. Same thing they pull on us." Laura took a sip of the tea she had purchased. "You could write that. After all, you *are* in the advertising business."

John smiled back. "I'll work on it."

"So how do we get them to actually come to it? We'd need to find a space."

John paused for a moment, then his eyes widened.

"Maybe we could find another convention going on at the same time. Tell them that that convention is just a *cover* for their convention. After all, what good spammer would show up at a place to be caught?"

"I like the way you think. I'll check to see what's going on in March. That should give us enough time to send out the emails and get their responses."

For the remainder of the afternoon, Laura showed John some of her favorite places to go in the city. They strolled along the many scenic trails in Papago Park until they ended up at the Desert Botanical Garden. John asked if he could take her picture next to a giant saguaro cactus. He would look at that picture often throughout the week.

Laura prided herself on being an excellent researcher. Many times her duties at the law firm required her to scour the Internet for comparable cases and their legal outcomes. The next day she came across an incident with a urologist, Dr. Eugene Benson, who was called to testify over improperly prescribed erectile-dysfunction medication. Turned out that the patient just wanted to see how much longer they could maintain an erection by taking several pills at once. Dr. Benson was also the organizer of the

2022 Urologists Convention in Las Vegas on the last weekend of March. Laura gave him a call.

He confided that one of the biggest complaints among urologists was the proliferation of imitation ED drugs on the web. The makers of Viagra, Cialis, and Vydox had new competition with Priapus, an untested and cheaper version of the other drugs that promised to sustain longer and harder erections. At least that's what the SPAM email claimed. It got its name from the Greek god of fertility, whose permanently erect and grotesquely large penis became his most-depicted attribute.

Dr. Benson welcomed the chance to get back at those responsible for patient confusion and lost prescription sales. Laura couldn't wait to share the news with John.

The following Friday, Laura met John at Marciano's Ristorante in Scottsdale for dinner. It was John's treat.

"I've got some good news," John announced after the server brought them their menus and water. "We've received two hundred and fifty replies to our 'I'm interested' email. They're on the hook."

"That's wonderful!" Laura sipped her water. "I think you're going to like what I found out. The 2022 Urologists Convention is meeting March 26-27 in Vegas. I spoke to the organizer, a Dr. Eugene Benson. He wants to work with us on our *project*. He said doctors suffer from bogus medications sold on the web and hawked through SPAM emails."

John chuckled for a moment. "A urologist convention. A suitable place for those scumbags to find themselves. They're the piss of the earth."

"He even suggested a hotel for us to send them to. He's arranging it so each one can share a room with an attending physician. We can make that part of the cover we talked about. They will *actually* be at a different convention so no one will suspect, except us and the doctors."

John was taken with the way Laura described her findings. This girl had spunk. Her eyes lit up when she spoke, but she still retained that homespun sensibility he had seen in Rachel. Pretty, too. She wore her long brown hair up in a bun with a few strands curling around the sides of her face. Her slender, voluptuous body was concealed by an orange and green one-piece dress. She looked like an understated vixen who could break out into her superhero persona at any moment.

For his part, he felt like the male half to those great male-female duos you see in the movies and TV: Harry to Hermione in *Harry Potter*, Mulder to Scully in *The X-Files*, and John to Jane in *Mr. and Mrs. Smith*. Bonnie and Clyde they were, indeed.

The waiter brought over the bottle of wine John had ordered: a rich, bloodred Cabernet Sauvignon.

"A toast to our skillful pairing. We shall bring these spammers to a merciless end. Blood shall pour, much like that within our goblets."

Laura laughed at John's medieval warrior impersonation, then took a long sip of the tart wine. Her wheels were still spinning.

"We should charge for the convention. Say also that they must bring their laptops and cell phones as proof of their spamming activities. That way we can get a list of their victims."

"Excellent idea, my lady." John tried to shy from his upfront reply. The quick buzz from the wine had loosened his lips. But Laura winked back, much to his surprise. "I will work on the website over the weekend," he followed.

Over dinner Laura told him about her life growing up in Michigan. She, too, had a Midwestern upbringing. They both longed for the change of seasons. Their respective careers had taken them to the Southwest. Many of John's clients were in Phoenix, but some were as far away as Dallas and Chicago. Laura left for Arizona to be near her sick mother, who passed away in 2011. Her long hours at the law firm kept her from traveling—one of her biggest goals in life. Now that her savings had disappeared, those plans were more out of reach than ever. John promised he'd help her get back on track. For now he kept secret that he had also received a response from the person who sent her the phishing email. It wasn't the right time.

Dr. Benson had a secret of his own.

For nearly twenty years he had built up his practice in San Antonio, Texas. He even pioneered the development of new drugs that shortened, and often prevented, acute urinary tract infections. But the ins and outs of...ins and outs...had grown tiresome.

He'd seen a lot of dicks in his life: big ones, little ones, skinny ones, thick ones. Men longed for a pill that would do more than just pump blood into their flaccid cocks for a few hours. That's all the existing drugs did. Not one enhanced their libido at the same time. Having sex with the aid of erectile-dysfunction medication had the eroticism of sticking a round peg into a round hole. There was no rage in their hard-ons. Dr. Benson saw an unmet need.

He covertly began a consortium with other urologists to develop a drug that could supersize a man's cock and his libido simultaneously. Even highly potent men wanted to see how much further they could go in terms of size and sexual stamina. Priapus Plus (PP), jokingly referred to by his colleagues as the Pee-Pee drug, was the code name. He wanted to stretch the limits, literally.

So he began the formulation, which was a combination of the knockoff Priapus, and extracts from various plants in the Amazon known to stimulate male testosterone production. Tests on lab rats showed that different species of rats reacted differently to early versions of the drug. He concluded that different ethnicities of the human male might also respond accordingly. An Asian male might need a different formulation than an Indian male, for instance. Only after he had determined the right combinations and dosages of the medication for a large cross-section of the population would he put the product on the market.

What he lacked were test subjects.

John called Laura on Wednesday night to direct her to the faux website he had created for the 2022 Spammer Convention. It was a simple but sophisticated design, which included a translation button up top so spammers around the world could understand it. Bullets highlighted the convention topics: Bulk Emailing, Effective IP Masking, and Discreet Bank Transfers. A payment form required full disclosure of their real names and credit card numbers so monetary awards could be matched up with their spamming logs.

"I'm charging $500 a pop for admission. That should weed out the not-so-successful spammers. They also have to submit their income from spamming over the past year. Prizes will be matched on their success."

"That's fantastic!" Laura scrolled through the site. "This looks so good I think I'd fall for it." She laughed. John was hoping she would fall for something else—him, to be specific. Images of her at the restaurant had stirred him out of his sleep every night since. That alluring smile, those seductive eyes, those firm breasts. In his dreams she was Angelina Jolie from *Tomb Raider* pulling him up from his mattress to help her locate the Triangle of Light. He quickly composed himself.

"I've included the hotel they are required to stay at: the Johnson Inn on Sierra Avenue. That's correct, right?"

"Yes. I spoke to Dr. Benson and he said he and the other urologists will cover the room charges, since each spammer will be paired with a doctor."

"Where would you like to stay? Should we stay in the same hotel or—" John didn't want her answer to spoil his fantasy.

"Let me do some checking around tomorrow." Laura hadn't thought that far ahead. "Let's get together at the cafe on Saturday. Will you be free?"

"Absolutely. I'm beginning to like that little place." He wasn't about to pass up a chance to see her again. "Two o'clock sound good?"

"OK, I'll see you then. Good night, *John*." The tone of her voice had a trace of tease to it. The way she said his name, slow and specific. It took all he could muster not to dive into the suggestive back-and-forth he'd have with women on MatchnMeet: What are you wearing? Where do you like to be touched? How big do you want it?

"Good night (*don't say my lady*). Good night, Laura."

Laura lay in bed for an hour after their conversation. She looked over the website again, noting the cunning verbiage and tactical graphic placement. The man did have a way with words. She rubbed her fingers lightly over the screen as if she were caressing his smooth, muscled chest. The weekend couldn't come soon enough.

Meanwhile, Dr. Benson began contacting all the attending urologists with special instructions on what to bring and where to stay. In just two weeks they would make significant progress in one fell swoop. "It's going to be a wild night, ladies and gentlemen," was how he ended his email.

John paced back and forth outside of the cafe that Saturday afternoon. He had arrived an hour early. It was a balmy eighty degrees, warm enough to wear his jogging shorts and a tank top.

At precisely two, Laura appeared along the narrow walk in front of the line of shops that led to the cafe. Her flowing, strapless summer dress revealed her taut arms. Her hair was down from the usual bun and grazed the top of her shoulders. Her eyes lit up when she spotted John, who had propped himself up against a street lamp the moment he saw her approaching.

"Hi, you look very nice." John's smile couldn't get much wider.

"Thank you, just something I got on sale last spring. It's such a beautiful day out."

"Just perfect. Shall we eat outside?"

"I'd like that, yes."

John pulled out one of the metal chairs on the patio for Laura to sit in. He returned from inside a few minutes later with a couple of iced teas and one of Laura's favorite chocolate-filled pastries.

"I have some terrific news." John sat in the chair next to her and tapped away at his tablet screen.

"What's that?" Laura pulled the cold iced tea up to her lips and took a long sip.

"Well, I sent out emails directing the spammers to our website. So far close to one hundred have registered. I think we're up to ninety-two."

"You're kidding!" Laura leaned toward John to look at the screen. It felt as if her head was in his lap. "And they all paid?"

"Yep. That's $46,000 in the bank, so far. I think your money worries are over."

"Oh my God, I can't believe we are pulling this off. And the money is all good? Nothing fraudulent?"

"I checked this morning. Everything is fine. I withdrew it into a separate account so there's no way they can hack into it and take it back."

Laura noticed the muscles in John's bare arms as he placed the tablet back onto the table. His chest pressed against the inside of his tank, pushing the fabric out as far as it could stretch. The back of her neck wept beads of perspiration.

"Read me the email you sent; I want to hear how crafty you were." What she really wanted was to see those arms flex again when he picked up the tablet. As he read the email aloud, she watched his lips move. He had stopped shaving the week before, and a fine shadow of dark black hair was settling in on his jowl and upper lip. She pulled the glass of tea up to her lips and held it there to conceal her beguiling smile. This man was certainly attractive.

After John finished, he looked over to Laura with a hesitant smile. "What are we going to do with them once they arrive, aside from pairing them with the doctors?"

"Don't worry about that. All we have to do is retrieve their computers and smartphones. Dr. Benson said he and the others will take it from there." She sipped the iced tea, then bit into the pastry. A speck of cream oozed out onto the side of her mouth. John grabbed a napkin and gently wiped it away.

"Don't want to get that pretty dress dirty." Laura grabbed his wrist as he pulled his arm back, then slowly let her hand trail down to his.

"I can't thank you enough. This means a lot to me."

John smiled and reached for his tea with his other hand.

"We make a good team."

It was hard to break away from that moment, but the cafe suddenly bustled with new patrons. The din of chairs moving and people discussing their weekend plans crept inward. The two shared a smile, then began a conversation of their own. Laura said she had never been to Hawaii, though she often sent correspondence there through her job. John imagined her doing the hula in that dress, or something a little more revealing to show off her midriff. He talked about traveling to South America for an Amazon expedition. She imagined him pulling her up into a large treehouse like Tarzan.

They left the cafe two hours later. She would book their room across the street from the Johnson Inn at the classier Sierra Grande Hotel. John walked her back to her car, wanting more than ever to kiss her on the lips. Being apart for two weeks was going to be painful.

On the day of the convention, both Laura and John separately drove the three hundred miles from Phoenix to Vegas. It took every ounce of concentration for John not to accidentally drive off the road while thinking about seeing her again. When he arrived at the hotel, she had already left a note with the hotel attendant:

John, the event is on the first floor of the Harris Convention Center two blocks south of the hotel. I'll be sitting at a table directly opposite from the urologist's table, just like we planned. See you soon, Laura.

It was just after noon when he joined Laura. The line for the fictitious 2022 Spammer Convention, abbreviated SPMC 2022 on the printed sign that draped over the check-in table, looked like a trail of immigrants who just stepped onto Ellis Island: Asians, Indians, Africans, Russians, and a few Americans. All males. Each was asked to leave his laptop and smartphone in the corner after Laura applied a sticker to the devices that included their names and spreadsheet record number.

"It looks like we got the mother load here," John whispered to Laura.

"I know," she whispered back. He could smell her fresh, apricot-scented hair when she leaned in. "How many registered total?"

"One hundred and fifty have paid. "

"Oh wow. There are three hundred urologists at the convention. I'll tell Dr. Benson so they can pair two doctors with one spammer per table."

"Do you have any idea what he's going to do with them?"

"I don't know, but I think we will soon find out."

The last person to check in with John was Onyango Ohingo, the man who hacked into Laura's bank account. After he handed John his ticket, John nodded to Dr. Benson, who met Onyango at the door and ushered him into the large room. It was at precisely 2:00 p.m. when the event began. Dr. Benson moved to the podium in front of the room.

"Ladies, Gentlemen, thank you for coming to the 2022 Urologists Convention. My respected colleagues, please welcome our guests at your tables. They've been kind enough to join us at our event." The doctors greeted each of the unsuspecting crooks while a group of servers delivered glasses of water to each table. The slightly larger glasses with numbers stamped on the bottoms were carefully positioned in front of the spammers. Laura and John sat near the front of the room at a table of their own.

A minute later, a gigantic penis projected onto the overhead screen.

"Big cocks are big business," continued Dr. Benson, whose statement drew a chuckle from the room. "Current medication simply doesn't cut it. That's why, as you know, I've been working on a formula that will not only increase the size of the penis, but will also enhance the male libido. There's stiff competition out there (another laugh) and so we have to head them off, so to speak."

Laura and John snickered a bit and exchanged a furtive glance. The screen flipped to a schematic of the full male body with a pill entering its mouth.

"One of the other drawbacks of current medication is that a single pill may not achieve the desired results. We want users to be able to control the size of their erection with the dosage they take." A graph displayed with number of pills on the bottom axis and enlarging penises as the vertical bars. "For instance, a single pill could force, say, four tablespoons or sixty milliliters of blood into the penis to extend it an inch. Two pills would extend it two inches, et cetera."

Twenty minutes into the talk, the spammers seemed a bit agitated. Laura leaned into John.

"They were told that the prizes would be awarded to the best spammers at the end of event. Right?"

"Yes, that's correct." John paused for a moment. "I have something to tell you. You see the guest sitting at Dr. Benson's table?"

Laura tilted her head to look across the room.

"That tall black man?"

"Yep. His name is Onyango Ohingo. He responded to the email that was sent to you."

"You mean he's the one who stole my money?" Laura looked back at the man, who abruptly slipped his left hand under the table.

"I would assume so. I contacted Dr. Benson on my own and arranged for him to sit at his table. I know what they're going to do—"

Before he could finish, a shout rang out in the middle of the room. An Asian man was grasping the edge of his table with both hands as if he might float away. His eyes bugged out. Another shout, more like a cry of agony, echoed in the back of the room. There a man of Indian descent shot both his hands under the table and rested them between his thighs.

"What's happening?" Laura looked over to John.

"The time has come, my colleagues," Dr. Benson continued. "The time has come for us to reap the benefits of our hard work. Our guests have flown here from all around the world. Look at them. These are the men who have hawked our drugs, stolen our identities, and done everything possible to undermine the hard work we have done as doctors. I can tell you first hand that I receive at least half a dozen emails a day for knockoff erectile-dysfunction medication."

By now many of the men had simply fallen to the floor. Large bulges pressed out from the front of their pants, which they frantically struggled to conceal.

"Men. Make no effort to fight it. Your water contains a magic potion to make your cocks big, Big, BIG—or however you'd word that in your emails. Each of you has received a different dosage of our new drug, Priapus Plus. Some, just one pill. Others, well, let's just say that the human skin is quite elastic."

Several of the men began humping the carpeted floor like horned-up caterpillars. Others appeared to be masturbating while attempting to readjust themselves.

Laura put her hand up to her mouth to conceal her laughter.

"Right now I would imagine many of you could fuck a horse. It's probably quite excruciating, all that pressure down there. But, let me say that you've come to the right place. Our esteemed urologists will be escorting you back to the hotel rooms. There they will administer medication to relieve your suffering. We mustn't waste time. Doctors, you may proceed."

The writhing men were scooped up and walked to the back door and into a bus where they were transported to the hotel. John and Laura remained with Dr. Benson, who thanked them for their efforts.

"A job well done. We'll take it from here. You have everything you need?"

"Yes," Laura replied. "We'll contact the authorities to pick up the laptops and phones so they can locate their other victims. What will happen to those men, especially the man who sat at your table? He was the one who took my money."

"I can assure you that these men will never see the light of day again. Let's just say that they will be making invaluable contributions to the medical establishment."

"C'mon, Laura." John put his arm around her shoulder. "Let's freshen that bank account of yours." After they gathered their belongings, the two walked hand-in-hand back to their hotel.

"You are now the recipient of $75,000," said John while tapping away at his tablet at the edge of the hotel bed.

"Oh, John. I can't take all of that. Let's split it."

"No, no. It's all yours. I think I got what I wanted. Just spending time with you was payment enough."

Laura crawled onto the bed and began rubbing his shoulders. As she kneaded the base of his neck, she remembered thinking what a catch he was the moment they met at the cafe. John felt her soft and tender hands slide down the sides of his biceps. He turned and their lips instantly met. It was a soft kiss at first, then they parted and looked into each other's eyes. There was no more fear or apprehension. John laid the tablet on the stand and turned back to her, this time embracing Laura tightly within his sinewy arms. They immediately fell onto the bed and settled in for a deeper kiss.

Back at the Johnson Inn, the pairs of doctors had already sedated the spammers. There wasn't much time to extract the necessary data from the first human trials of Priapus Plus. Penis lengths and girths were carefully measured with precision instruments. Some had elongated as much as eighteen inches with testicles the size of tennis balls.

John rolled Laura in their embrace until he hovered over her. Their hands clasped above her head as he kissed the curve of her neck. She felt the coarse bristles on his face glance over her skin. It made her quiver. A minute later he sat up and pulled off his shirt. She reached out and dragged the tips of her fingers down between his pecs and along the ripples of his abs.

Scalpels slit deep and scissors snipped away at tissues. It was imperative that the subjects be alive while their body parts were harvested. Onyango came to as Dr. Benson traced a dotted line with a marker just above his cock. Both his hands and legs were restrained to the hotel bed atop a plastic drop cloth. Thick duct tape covered his mouth to muffle his screams. Dr. Benson reached for the serrated scissors.

John's firm hands delicately peeled away Laura's blouse. She helped with the last button, then grabbed for his belt. He looked up to the ceiling and closed his eyes as she slipped her hand inside the front of his pants.

His eyes rounded with terror when Dr. Benson made the first snip. "This will hurt you more than it will hurt me," the doctor chided. Onyango buckled in agony.

73

"Well, I see someone *certainly* doesn't need a pill." Laura gripped John's cock and pulled it over the top of his pants. He pushed the denim to his knees and surrounded her hands with his. His mind raced with pleasurable thoughts.

Tears dripped from Onyango's eye sockets with each laceration. Blood spilled out into a pan between his thighs. Dr. Benson eyed his work like a rancher castrating a bull. It just needed to be done.

Laura removed her skirt after John unclasped her bra. This gorgeous woman now lay before him fully naked. Her breasts were as beautiful as he had imagined. He leaned in to kiss them, then drifted his lips back up to hers. She bit down lightly the moment he entered her.

The last snip completely separated Onyango's cock from his body. Dr. Benson banded up the cut end of the engorged member, then manipulated it in his gloved hands like an animal wrangler showing off a thick eel. "This is quite impressive." He held it up for Onyango to see. The man's eyes screamed panic. The doctor lowered the severed cock into a cooler of ice.

John and Laura undulated as the sweat dripped off their bodies and onto the crisp sheets. She screamed out his name several times, which drove him mad.

Dr. Benson proceeded to remove Onyango's head. Back at the lab he would measure the amount of drug secreted into the brain's cortex and compare it with the Priapus Plus dosage received. "Two heads are better than one," he said as he began cutting away. Blood instantly gushed from Onyango's neck once the electric knife pierced his skin. His pleading grunts were silenced after the blade sliced through his vocal cords. His eyes rolled upward just before his fully separated head rolled to its side. Dr. Benson quickly wrapped it in plastic and placed it into the cooler. This was the scene repeated room after room.

Twenty minutes later Laura and John collapsed onto each other, fully spent and completely satisfied. He put his arm around her as the two rested on their backs and stared into the spinning ceiling fan. Their breathless panting soon turned to laughter, and eventually, they fell into a peaceful sleep with her head upon his chest.

Dr. Benson handed a large bill to the nighttime attendant, who helped the others carry the coolers and the corpses to a waiting truck. One hundred and fifty specimens was a very good start. At least now, the doctor thought, he had a disposable resource for human trials. No one would suspect, and no one would care.

****

Six seconds was all it took for John and Laura to seal their relationship with a kiss on the northern beach of Maui, the spot they chose for their wedding one year later. Their new home was a quaint Victorian in Lowell, Indiana. John became the head marketing director at a Chicago advertising firm, which was awarded the Priapus Plus campaign. Mocking Cialis' tame silhouette of a couple holding hands in two side-by-side clawfoot tubs, the Priapus Plus commercials ended with a silhouette of a couple clawing *at* each other.

Laura opened a small boutique just west of town that specialized in locally produced clothing, housewares, and decor. Everything was discounted, of course, including the little pink pills at the register that kept the men of Lowell quite happy and the women of Lowell eternally satisfied.

PEOPLE WHO NEED TO DIE

Internet Trolls

I hope you die.
You're a faggot. Faggot.
You're fat and really, really ugly.
Your voice sounds like rocks in a blender.
Liberals are to blame. F*ck you, liberals.
Go stand in traffic and kill yourself.
Your opinion doesn't matter.
Why don't you just fade away?
You suck! Don't quit your day job.
I'll say whatever I want. First Amendment, baby.

The letters, the words, the short, clunky sentences. The long-winded diatribes in which you become king—to yourself. Meant to jab, meant to stab, meant to grab attention. You certainly *do* get to the point.

You can be elusive, though. Sneaky is the better word. You wait for the right moment. No need to give yourself away, just yet. Why not let it build, so you can knock it all down. Or you can just peck, peck, *peck* away. There are so many ways, and you'll try them all.

I can see you, because you want to be seen. In fact, you couldn't live without me. I'm the food that feeds your need. But it's all external, really. Because you have nothing inside.

I'm the conscience that you don't have, reflected in the people you try to hurt.

****

Mary Beth Higgins had just spent four long years working on her memoir. In it, she detailed the sexual abuse she had suffered as a child. No names were mentioned; she wasn't that type of person. Instead, she explained that the predator was "a friend of the family." In truth, it was her sister's boyfriend.

She was nine at the time. She had just entered the fourth grade at Langdon Elementary in Tacoma, Washington. Her sister, Natalie, was a junior at Langdon High. Though there was a seven-year age difference, and a puberty gap that gifted Natalie with a body that all the boys desired, the sisters remained close. So close that every Sunday afternoon Natalie would take young Mary Beth to a matinee show at the Grand Theatre on Dover Street. Movies were only fifty cents back in 1959, and it allowed them to connect outside of the busy school week. It was those cherished afternoons, when innocence met adventure and intrigue, that spawned the four-decade movie career of which Mary Beth also wrote about.

Fame was something she never planned. It happened so gradually that it wasn't until after her eighth movie, *Serenade in the Park*, that the public took notice. By then Hollywood reporters discovered that scandals sold more rags than critical movie reviews. Her husband was a major player in the industry, known to be quite the starlet chaser. That's when the world discovered her, the woman who always seemed to play second fiddle to the more glamorous stars of the time: the best friend, the concerned neighbor, the confidante. Now she was on the covers of *National Enquirer* and *Star*. It was unwelcome publicity, but directors took notice. She soon received more prominent roles, and everyone wanted to know more about the enigmatic woman with the sultry blue eyes.

She retired from moviemaking in 2010 at age 60. She and her husband settled down in the hills outside San Bernardino, where she remained at his side until he breathed his last breath in the winter of 2015. They had one daughter together, Samantha, who moved to New York City in her twenties to pursue her own dreams of stardom.

Her sister Natalie passed away in 2017 of ovarian cancer. Despite decades of research and billions of dollars of funding, there was still no cure for the deceptive disease. She never told Natalie about the young man who sodomized her in her childhood bedroom. That's because Natalie married him four years later and began raising a family of her own. Mary Beth feared that if she confided in Natalie about what had been done to her, Natalie may never speak to her again. She could lose the one person who meant the most to her.

What if he did the same thing to his own children? She couldn't bear to think about it. It took her years to get that image out of her mind, that sinister look that crawled over his face each time he'd touch her on her bed. He'd slip in while Natalie was getting ready for one of their nights out, acting as though he was playing Barbies with her little sister while she showered and picked out her clothes. He'd point to parts of the doll and ask nine-year-old Mary Beth to point to the same parts on her own body. And then he'd do it for her. He'd tell her to show him where parts of the Ken doll were on him. Sometimes he'd hold her tiny hand over his crotch and make her rub it. Then he'd do more, much more. And he warned her to never tell Natalie or it might make her sister really mad that they had this *special* bond together.

It was a painful experience to relive for her autobiography, even if it ended sixty years ago. It was something she had never told anyone, not even her husband. But the book was about her life, and as in her movies, she intended to write about it with the same conviction and authenticity she gave to her on-screen roles. She just hid who it was.

That man, her brother-in-law, perished one year before the book was published. She knew he was on his way out when her niece sent her an email about her father's illness. Lung cancer. That's what took him. Mary Beth desperately wanted to know if Anna had experienced the same trauma as she had. But Anna's letters were always polite and upbeat, and her husband, Douglas, was very much a gentleman. The two always sent her roses on her birthday, and they'd tell her what a beautiful actress she was when her movies aired on the classic movie channels. She didn't want to upset Anna, because doing so would be betraying her mother. And the two looked so much alike.

Mary Beth's autobiography, *A Hidden Life*, skyrocketed to #1 on best-seller lists just two weeks after its release. Many asked how she was able to get through such an ordeal and still trust men. Even more so to marry one of the most powerful in Hollywood, a known cheater, and stay with him. But others, the Internet trolls, lashed out at her for not naming the abuser. They judged her, and they judged her harshly.

"I hope you rot in hell for your silence."

"Another washed-up actress using sexual molestation as a publicity stunt to sell books."

"How many other victims did you open the doors for?"

"Shameful, just like your movies."

A coalition of haters started online groups explicitly targeting Mary Beth for her choices. "The Enabler," they called her. All were encouraged to give her biography a one-star rating and to write something bad about it, even if they'd never read it. They seemed to pride themselves on how mean-spirited they could be. Those with the cruelest words were awarded additional "likes."

There's one thing about artists, whether they're actors or musicians, painters or poets, authors or artisans, or performers on a stage: they care what people think. And more often than they should, they bemoan the opinions of those who didn't like their work. These are the ones they'll remember.

Seventy-one-year-old Mary Beth had spent most of her life lamenting her past, and now she would discover, in her final days, that others wanted her to suffer even more. Sure, she had endured fair criticisms of her movies, but to read the most hurtful things about something so personal was more than she had anticipated. Where was this hostility coming from, and how many of these commenters were abused themselves to make such judgments? She could never understand how those she'd tried to entertain would ultimately choose her own sorrow for their enjoyment.

On May 12, 2021, Mary Beth died in her bedroom in the quaint, two-story Fontana condo she had purchased after her husband passed. She left all her assets to Anna.

It was a gift, his mother would tell him. It made him unique and special. From the moment he could recognize his reflection in the mirror, she let him know that the small protrusion on the right side of his head must have been heaven sent. "God doesn't make mistakes," she'd say. And for a while, he believed her.

Somehow the kids at school saw it differently. Like in the first grade when little Sarah Robinson walked over to him on the playground and asked him straight out.

"Why you got no ear?" she said in her thimble of a voice.

"I got an ear. It's just smaller than the other one," Jeremy replied.

In fact, it was much smaller, and quite deformed. A mere triangular flap, like a mini Post-it cut along the diagonal and stuck to his head. Like a dog-eared book page, which, unfortunately, ended up being his nickname at Clover Elementary.

"Hey, little dog ear," the other kids would say.

For his first three years of school, Jeremy would dash home in tears at least once a week. Eventually, he learned to ignore the taunts, telling the other kids that he had extraordinary hearing in that ear, like a superhero. Did they? Unfortunately, that was not the case. Along with the outside, his right inner ear hadn't fully developed. The cochlea could barely pick up sounds below the volume of a passing fire truck, or Sarah Robinson's piercing scream the day she reached out and touched his "gift from God." He heard that sound, loud and clear.

His family couldn't afford a prosthetic to at least conceal it from view. Instead, he let his hair grow out in an effort to cover it up. But he knew he was different, and no matter how much he tried to hide it from others, he could never hide it from himself.

Then he learned he did, indeed, have a special gift. He could tell stories with pictures.

At the local Goodwill one day, Jeremy discovered an old digital camera in the used-electronics section. He begged his mother to get it for him. It was a Nikon, three megapixels, circa 2004. Not good enough to produce large prints, but perfect for the moviemaker program on the old HP desktop PC his father had pulled out of the basement and fired up for him. The program allowed Jeremy to create intriguing slideshows with slow pans and zooms, plus add narration and titles. Nearly every rich kid in school had those same capabilities on their smartphones, but what they lacked was Jeremy's sense of wonder. It was his storytelling that made his videos special.

The first was an exposé on the different insects he found in the yard one afternoon. He captured images of bees and butterflies, beetles and ants, and spiders and katydids. He even discovered a baby walking-stick bug camouflaged by the bark on an old elm tree. In the video piece he put together he asked, "What do bugs think of us?" And it was something he really wanted to know.

"Do they like us?" he'd narrate. "Are they always afraid of us? When I put my finger next to a beetle, it sometimes stops before climbing onto it. Did it make up its mind that I was okay? Does it want to be my friend?"

In his next video he gave voices to the various items of clothing hanging out on the line one day. His mother's red blouse was Queen Katherine, who was married to his father's faded blue jeans, also known as King Levi. An army of white cotton socks, which appeared to be marching as they swayed back and forth between the two parallel clotheslines, protected the village of undergarments.

Jeremy's father helped set up a Youtube account for this son, and once uploaded, the first two videos were shared many times over. But it was the next one that would set an Internet record.

After talking to Mr. Dean, an old man who sat outside Ditman's convenience store on Bradley Road every day, Jeremy decided to make a video about all the physical abnormalities that make people special. Mr. Dean had a missing finger on his left hand.

"I was a young lad, probably no more than a few years older than you at the time," he spoke into Jeremy's microphone. "My Pa told me he needed more kindling for the fire, and so he sent me outside to retrieve some. Well, there really wasn't much scrap wood left, just a few pieces of bark and such at the base of the stack. So I took a narrow log, grabbed the nearby ax, and chopped into it. The second hit cut clear through my index finger. I actually thought it was a splinter of wood, until I saw the blood. I screamed so loud that I woke up the neighbors. Lucky for me Mr. Davidson was also a doctor, and he fixed me up good."

Jeremy interviewed more of his neighbors. Mrs. Smith had patchy brown spots on her arms, and her left eye wandered a bit. Penny Trudeau, the girl next door, had a small scar on her knee from when her bike hit a rock in the road and threw her off. Ten stitches it took. Leroy Sams lost his right leg in one of the wars. Paul Babcock had a boil on his foot that got infected or something, so they had to remove his big toe. And newborn Tamitha Yoder had a cleft lip.

To finish up the piece, Jeremy took pictures of himself and spoke about his ear. He even included images of when he was a baby. He talked about how it had affected his hearing, too. And that there really wasn't much that doctors could do because they had no money.

The video was an instant viral hit. After a week it had over ten million views. Many of the comments were supportive, commending the people who took part for sharing their stories. But an equal number were not.

"Ick. That's just gross!" some would say, or in more explicit words.

"A video of misfit people. Maybe you all need to be sent off to some island or something to die together."

"Can you *hear* me? LOL."

But the one that hurt the most, the words that probably took the troll no more than ten seconds to write before he, or she, moved on to the next victim, stayed with young Jeremy.

"No matter how talented you are with your videos, people will always look at your lopsided head and think, this guy's a freak!"

It was like the fan who spotted a young, acned Michael Jackson with his brothers at an airport and exclaimed, "Eww, what happened?" And we know how that ended. Words carry weight, and for some, that weight can be too much to bear.

On June 23, 2021, Jeremy hung himself from the same elm tree where he discovered the walking-stick bug just a few months earlier. He was eight years old.

Very little had been done in the Internet community among social media sites to curb abusive commenting and bullying. The fact was, there was just too much of it to control. Self-regulation was ineffective; trolls would just gang up and flag innocent commenters for unsubstantiated wrongdoing. Or they'd create new accounts each time they got banned. And there was always that First Amendment thing. Perhaps it needed an amendment itself.

But trolls could also be nice. Sometimes, a little *too* nice.

Nice enough to make you believe they were in love with you.

Sandy Greenwood was a nineteen-year-old sophomore at Radison Community College in Wisconsin, when an online interest professed his love for her. The man, whose screen name was JacktheLover, declared that after two months of back and forth exchange, he really adored Sandy. Maybe they could meet during summer break.

Jack was a twenty-two-year-old senior at the University of Wisconsin at OshKosh, where he was completing his degree in Sports Medicine. He was also a star athlete on the Titan football team. And he was extremely attractive. Muscles, yes, he had a lot of them. Ripped abs, muscled calves, wide shoulders—everything a woman could want. Plus he was sharp as a tack.

All of Sandy's dorm friends drooled over the pictures he'd send her throughout the week. His messy brown hair, shadowed scruff, and brilliant smile made the girls swoon. And he really loved everything about her, too.

"You have such a pretty face. I can't wait to kiss it," he'd write to her.

"You're too kind," she'd reply.

The fact is, Sandy did have a pretty face. And she'd heard that compliment many times before. But she also knew the well-intentioned comment was usually reserved for fat people. It was another way of saying, "Your body is ugly, but your face is nice."

And, admittedly, she knew she was overweight. Thirty pounds over, according to the charts in the Health and Wellness class she was taking. Weight that seemed to hitch a ride on her ass and thighs the moment she left home. All those late-night Domino's stress binges before midterms and finals were probably the cause. Or it could have been the boyfriend from high school that dumped her just after graduation. However it got there, it didn't seem to want to part with her no matter how many miles she walked to classes every day. But Jack reassured Sandy that she was extremely beautiful to him.

"Don't change a thing. I like you how you are."

Now, Sandy was no fool. She was going to make sure this Jack guy was legit. So she went online and compared the pictures he'd sent with Google Image search results. Sure enough, it came up with Jack Mosbey, quarterback for the Titans in the 2020-2021 football season. His major was listed as Sports Medicine, with an emphasis on injury rehabilitation. And all the pictures he'd sent her of him were candid shots. Most appeared to be selfies.

How could she have doubted him?

Dialogue between the two reached a peak in late May, just a few weeks before final exams. Jack had asked her to send a few nude shots so he could "make it through finals with a smile on his face." He had already sent her a couple of faceless shots with his football pants pulled down to his knees, exposing his thick, hairy thighs and a substantial endowment.

"See what you do to me?" he commented on the photo. "Now, when you take your pictures, don't hide your face. I want to see that perfect body and beautiful face together. It would make me so happy."

She hesitated, but she also didn't want to disappoint him by saying no. If he loved her down to the bare essentials, then he must really care for her. So she set up her iPhone when her roommate was out, put on her favorite silk panties, and took several pictures with her hair up in a bun. In the final photo she removed her panties, strategically hid her breasts and privates with her arms, and blew a Marilyn Monroe-esque kiss to the camera. Later that afternoon she excitedly emailed the pictures to him.

But there was no reply. Not that day, nor the next.

Then she started getting strange looks from the girls in her dorm. They'd giggle when they passed by her in the hallway. And that continued with others on campus. A few girls in her health class turned around and blew her a kiss two days before the final. It was a friend's text message that revealed what was going on. Her photograph had been leaked onto the school's social website.

She rushed home that Monday evening and saw her picture front and center, followed by pages of nasty comments.

"Moi, it's Ms. Piggy!"

"Bacon, bacon, bacon."

"I think I'm gonna barf!"

Sandy's roommate came back to find her in tears. School administrators removed the post by the end of the day, but it was too late. Hundreds of students had already copied and shared her naked selfie.

How did the picture get leaked? No one had access to her phone but her. The original poster used the screen name of JMosb. The account had just been opened with only the one post. Sandy sent off a scathing email to Jack Mosbey, which, again, went unanswered. It was her call to the University of Wisconsin football coach that set the media train in motion. Even though he professed his innocence in the matter, stating that he had never contacted Sandy, Jack was immediately suspended from the team.

A two-month investigation revealed the surprising culprit of the identity scam: Jack's younger brother, Jim. The twelve-year-old had purposely created the false online persona, using candid shots of his brother to catfish unsuspecting college girls. He was jealous of Jack for receiving the most attention in the family. Now two lives were irrevocably damaged. Jack sought to lie low for the summer. Sandy failed one of her classes and was unsure if she would return to college the following year.

Then she got an idea, and it would forever change the Internet.

Summer break was a time usually reserved for trips to the beach, backyard grilling, amusement parks, and full-blown dawdling. Some students worked long hours at summer jobs to pay for tuition. Instead, Sandy chose to invest her time in a little research project. She wanted to know what made trolls tick.

The Internet was the obvious place to start. Trolls, the kind that posted mean comments, enjoyed the anonymity of the exchange. It was something they'd never do in real life, as they would receive instant cues as to how it was affecting the other person. For that reason, Facebook and other social network sites had forced users to divulge their full name and background information. Comments they made would therefore be tied to their public identity. This drastically curbed trolling on those particular sites. But it also left a void. Where could trolls go to...troll?

She also studied why some trolls took it a step further and would choose to seduce others with false identities. Why would someone put the effort into obtaining fake photos, creating fake profiles, and interacting with someone they probably *did* want to meet at some point?

Low self-esteem. The obvious answer. Many trolls don't feel they are good-looking enough or smart enough to be with that other person. In the case of Jack's little brother, it was simply a matter of revenge catfishing. He had a vendetta.

The bigger question: how not to be lured into troll traps.

The oft-repeated rule, "Don't Feed The Trolls," inferred that if you didn't engage with them, they'd have no recourse for their discourse. Unfortunately, their unwelcome words would still appear in front of unwelcome eyes. And she knew it would be hard to get other online users to stop interacting with them.

Then Sandy thought, perhaps the solution wasn't in how to avoid troll traps, but how to lure trolls *away*. It would take the right bait, of course, as any good fisherman would know. And so she asked her father.

Travis Greenwood was a skilled troller, having received

several Master Angler awards for his tenacious pursuit of Northern Pike in the surrounding Wisconsin lakes. Just about every summer weekend he'd hoist his old blue aluminum boat onto the trailer and haul it off to some secret location. This particular weekend he'd deploy it at Goose Lake, where last time he spotted what he thought would be a record catch. Sandy decided to join him.

"My little girl, what's got you interested in fishing?" he asked as he pushed them away from shore and started the onboard motor.

"I just thought it would be fun to learn about what you do."

"Well, it's not much. It's more of a sit and wait game. But it brings me peace."

The two were silent for several minutes as Sandy's father maneuvered the boat around some weed beds and over to the eastern reaches of the lake. It was a beautiful day. The sunlight flickered off the small ripples of water along the sides of the boat. When they came to a stop near a patch of cattails, Travis reached for a fishing rod and opened up his tackle box.

"So how do you know which one of those to choose from," Sandy asked.

"Well, it's mostly trial and error. But then again, what catches one fish might not catch another. Soon you come to know what works the best."

"Do they like live bait, or those fake rubbery things?" Sandy pointed to the individual compartments inside the box.

"Doesn't matter, much. It's all about making them believe what's on the end of the hook is real. So when you troll, you see," he pulled out a small orange lure with a white feathered tail. At the end was a shiny silver blade. "This here will spin around the center when it's pulled through the water. It flashes and makes the fish think it's swimming."

"There are so many here." Sandy picked through a few.

"Yep, I got my minnows, Storm Crappies, Wiggle Warts,

Scum Frogs, Buzz Baits, Husky Jerks—"

Sandy laughed. "I know a lot about scum frogs and husky jerks."

Travis knew about the turmoil his daughter had gone through with the photo scandal. But he figured she had learned her lesson: not to share private things unless it's done in private and in person. He smiled to let her know he understood.

"Go ahead. Which one you want me to try?"

Sandy reached back into the box. She pulled out a plastic lure with silver scales and red and yellow highlights.

"That's my Zara Spook perch. It's meant for moving along the top of the water like an injured fish. You sure about that?"

"I don't know. It looks pretty to me." Sandy smiled.

"Okay then, let's give her a try."

Travis attached the lure to the end of his line and cast it out some twenty feet. Then he started the trolling motor and slowly guided the boat toward the center of the lake.

"How do you know where the fish will be?" Sandy asked.

"Fish go where they can feed, or where they have successfully fed in the past. They'll stay in that vicinity if there is a replenishable source of food."

"So the right bait and a guaranteed food supply is the trick?"

"True for about anything in life," her father said with a chuckle in his voice.

It wasn't more than thirty seconds later when an explosive splash behind the boat startled the two. Travis grabbed his rod just in time.

"Oh Mary! We got a bite!"

"You got one already?" Sandy shouted.

Her father reeled in a few feet of line. A large green fish jumped out of the water, its yellow-spotted body twisting a full 360 in mid-air like a skilled Olympic diver.

"Look at her!" Travis braced his feet under the inside edge of the boat.

"What is it, daddy?" Sandy shifted closer to him.

"It's a Northern, baby. And it's a big one."

The fish dove under the water, resurfacing every few seconds to thrash about.

"This one's gonna put up a fight!"

Travis wedged the end of the rod between his thighs and reached over with his free hand to shut off the trolling motor. Sandy got behind him and held onto his shoulders as he took in more line. Minutes went by while the two worked together.

"Oh, yeah. She's the one. This is a winner!" Travis grimaced as his aching hands cranked the casting reel.

"You got him, daddy!"

At that moment Sandy understood the thrill of the catch— what it must have felt like for Jack's younger brother to see her fall for his bait. But now she could envision him on the other end of the line, the hook lodged deep within his puckered mouth. She wanted those Internet scumbags biting and thrashing about like that fish in front of her.

"Grab the net, honey!" For a moment Sandy thought Inter*net*, until she saw where her father was pointing.

"See if you can scoop it into the net. Let me bring her in a few more feet."

The tip of his rod bowed over so sharply it looked as if it would snap in two.

"Okay, try it now."

Sandy reached over the side of the boat and dipped the net in the water. Once she positioned it under the fish, her father took it from her and set down his rod. Together they lifted the massive catch out of the lake.

"Whoa! She's a beauty."

"That was great, daddy!"

"I tell you what, my girl. Maybe you're onto something with that lure choice. I think I know what I'll be using next time."

After a minute of watching the giant pike flop about on the

boat floor, the two lifted the exhausted fish between them and snapped a selfie. Then Travis lowered the fish back into the water, gently holding on to it until it abruptly snapped its tail and disappeared into the dark depths of Goose Lake seconds later.

"Let someone else share in the fun." Travis put his arm around his daughter while the two snacked on sandwiches and watched the afternoon seagulls skim over the shoreline.

Sandy now had a plan of attack. But it would require a bit more investigation, and help from her tech-savvy neighbor.

Ethan Edwards was seven when his family moved in next door to the Greenwoods. Sandy was nine. They instantly formed one of those special bonds reserved for geeky boys and not-so-attractive girls. Of course, it's the geeks and the fair-looking girls who often grow up to be the more attractive of the bunch. Just go to your reunions. But that's beside the point. At seventeen Ethan was still a geek, and still living at home. He had just finished high school and had his choice of colleges beckoning at his doorstep: Harvard, MIT, Princeton, Dartmouth, and so on. Sandy knew she could count on Ethan to help her out.

The two met in Brandt Park on a late-June afternoon. It was the place they'd often go as kids to escape the bullies and talk about stuff. This time they would hash out bigger things.

"I'm sorry about what happened to you, Sandy." Ethan began.

"I guess it was more my fault," Sandy replied, embarrassed. "But I hope, with your help, we can prevent this from happening to anyone else."

"I'll do what I can. What do you have in mind?"

"What do you know about Internet trolls?"

"I know they're a nuisance. I know they say a lot of hurtful shit. They're assholes, really. I can't stand having to navigate through their mess. I hate seeing comment threads hijacked by their antics."

"I want to develop a place where trolls can go feed. Only,

they won't always be feeding on live bait."

"Like a website?"

"Like a bunch of websites. And groups, and anywhere their time can be soaked up. Places where they want to return often. Places they don't want to leave, so they leave the rest of us alone."

"Sorta like Troll Trappers?"

"Exactly!"

The two exchanged a familiar smile. They had done this before. It was back in fourth grade when they concocted clever ways to occupy the time of schoolyard bullies. Once they faked a hidden treasure in the woods behind Brandt Park. They had slipped a map inside Randy Blackburn's backpack, and it wasn't long before he and his posse of bad seeds were on the trail. It kept them out of everyone's hair for weeks. Randy freaked when he dug up the human skull where he had expected to find two hundred dollars in cash. But that's another story.

"Hey, I think I have something that might work." It was a project Ethan had begun back in the seventh grade. Just a few years before, in 2014, a computer software program developed in Russia dubbed "Eugene Goostman" had passed the Turing artificial intelligence test. The test, initiated in the 1950s by British mathematician Alan Turing, was devised to determine if at least thirty percent of human participants could be fooled into believing that they were communicating with a real person instead of a machine. In this case participants were asked if typed responses to their questions came from a computer, or from a thirteen-year-old Ukrainian boy.

Ethan knew you could fool almost anyone with simple, canned responses; so ever since then he had perfected his own version of a Turing program. This would be the ultimate test, and probably the best use for it.

The two spent the next four weeks working out the details of the code and the website designs. Sandy had a hand in the look-

and-feel, while Ethan worked on the internal structure. The sites and groups would be buried into the Deep Web, also known as the Deepnet. This was the vast underbelly of the Internet that standard search engines couldn't reach. Like the deep waters in which catfish roam, and the dark caves and ditches where mythical trolls abided, it was the perfect metaphor: a bottom dwelling for bottom feeders.

The Troll Trapping sites went live on August 1, 2021. The bait was straight forward, playing right into narcissistic troll mentality. "Be The Biggest Bad Ass on the Web" and "Real or Catfish?" were just a few of the tag lines used to lure them down under. Groups were pre-loaded with controversial subject matter known to spur hours of bantering: religion, politics, sexuality, and other hot topics. Trolls were rewarded by other trolls for the best comebacks, and they were also ranked by the number of responses per post. Ethan's Turing program egged respondents on with catch phrases known to initiate flame wars. "You just don't see how stupid you are" and "I really feel sorry for you" always seemed to re-ignite lagging conversations.

As for the catfish dating sites, the *goal* when they signed up was to determine if the person they were chatting with was real or fake. They had a month to decide. Truth be told (pun intended), Ethan's program played no part it in. Trolls simply feigned interest with the express purpose of seeming as real as possible to each other. It was an endless game of deception.

Slowly, but noticeably, trolls disappeared from public view like worms tunneling into moist muck. Like unwanted particles filtering through a sieve and into the garbage catch. They left the Yahoos, and the Youtubes, and the RealJocks, and the Goodreads, and all the millions of sites where troll behavior had once disrupted considerate and constructive discussions. There would be no more cyberbullies stealing the lives of the young and the innocent. No more envious haters plaguing the talented and the gifted. And no more fakes misleading the ones who longed for true love. Sandy and Ethan knew they couldn't stop bad people from being bad. But they could squander away their time.

And time became crucial to the two childhood friends as summer waned and decisions had to be made. Ethan would pick Dartmouth College for its pioneering Artificial Intelligence research program, but he would hold off for a year. Sandy would take a job as an assistant healthcare technician for the Jefferson County Outreach Clinic. The two would spend their evenings and weekends together conceiving even bigger plans for the Internet. Perhaps eradicating frivolous news stories about reality-TV stars?

"By the way, I like how you looked in that picture," Ethan said as he held Sandy's hand during one of their many evening strolls through their small town of Watertown, Wisconsin. "But then again, I've always thought you were beautiful."

****

While you sit at your board in your unkempt room, there is a life outside. A life where faces trump avatars, and real voices outshine masqueraders. You'll never know it, of course, for your incorrigible thoughts suspend you like a noose. An identity crisis, indeed.

Your fate is decided with every rotten keystroke. A cancer of vitriol already has you dying inside. Cells are breaking down as we speak. Chemicals will build up, arteries will clog, and stress will lacerate every organ. It may be slow, but it is assuredly so.

So toil in your bloodbath, spoil it for others. Because, you see, it's only a matter of time. There's no need to track your IP, find your home, and slit your throat.

You're already dead.

PEOPLE WHO NEED TO DIE

Horrible Bosses

When his parents spooned a side of broccoli onto his dinner plate one night, he screamed so loud it was as if a knife had just plunged into his heart. When his older sister sat on his tricycle, he bellowed so hard it nearly gave Mrs. Conner a heart attack. And when little Terrence Brown on the playground wouldn't throw him the ball, all the canines in the neighborhood dove into their doghouses to escape from the piercing cries.

Shouting was how he got attention. Four-year-old Finley Ross knew that a well-timed tantrum would always get him his way. Not once from the time of his birth did his parents ever set him straight with appropriate disciplinary action: a hand over the mouth, a slap to the butt, or better yet, solitary confinement. No, they just went along with every unwarranted outburst from their only child. He'll grow out of it, they'd say. But he never did.

That brat from hell would grow up to be another boss from hell. And his workers, their spouses, their kids, and nearly everyone he came in contact with would ultimately suffer. It's the trickle-down effect. Poor parenting produces poorly behaved adults.

Paul Cantor had just started on at Roland Construction as

head foreman. Twenty years in the business of building houses earned him the reputation as a strong leader who knew how to get things done. He met every budget, every time constraint, and every last-minute alteration. Engineers and architects put their full trust in him, and he never let them down.

That was when he worked in Seattle under more liberal circumstances. His bosses were forward-thinking entrepreneurs, the ones who pioneered the sustainable-housing craze. Every new project took on more meaning, whether it was constructing an entire solar-based community, or building efficient and environment-friendly mini-houses. What he did had lasting importance.

But in the fall of 2021 he transferred to rural North Carolina to be closer to his ailing father. Roland was the most successful construction firm in the area, having underbid almost all their competitors. But success didn't necessarily translate into happiness, and the twenty or more workers on his crew could attest to the one central reason: Finley Ross.

Finley was the designated project supervisor on the plot of giant box houses in which Paul was assigned. It was a new development several miles east of Raleigh where the nearest shopping center was twenty minutes away. They were way out in the boonies, and it often made it difficult to coordinate supply deliveries and work schedules. Still, Paul made concessions in his personal life to meet the requirements. It was the second week on the project when Finley and Paul would have their first confrontation.

"You need to take Tom and Pete off foundation prep and have them dig the central septic system." Finley caught Paul off guard as he exited his work trailer.

"Tom and Pete are my best concrete layers. I can have Joseph and Stan dig the trench for the tank."

"No, I want Tom and Pete operating the backhoes," Finley insisted.

"But that will put us behind. We have to wait a month for the cement to cure. If they're busy removing debris and digging holes, we'll be late on footings and foundation. Joe and Stan can't do that, and Roland wants framing to begin no later than November 1."

"I don't care what Roland says. *I'm* the project supervisor here. So do as I say." Finley shuffled away in his Cabela's Roughneck jacket, hefty-man khakis, and work boots that rose up over his pants to mid-calf. He looked like an overweight jungle explorer with a hard hat.

Paul broke the news to Tom and Pete, who were, nonetheless, also experienced backhoe operators. Joseph and Stan were let off the entire week it took to complete.

The next time Paul encountered an angry Finley was one week before Thanksgiving, though the days leading up to it were just as contentious.

"I need you to work through the holiday," said Finley while shifting a toothpick from one side of his mouth to the other. He had just finished an entire foot-long turkey and sauerkraut sub. Paul was at his computer on the opposite side of the trailer logging in his crew's hours.

"You've got to be kidding me." Paul peered up from his desk.

"Nope, sorry. Not kidding. You, and everyone but Stan. I need you to let Stan go."

"*What?* I can't do that. Stan is one of our best guys. Without him, who is going to run the supplies over? And these guys already put in overtime so they'd have a three-day weekend. I promised them."

"Well," Finley glared over at Paul like a bully making a lunch-money deal, "I guess you'll have to go back on your word. Tell them they can have a longer Christmas vacation."

"What is wrong with Stan?"

"I just don't like him. He's got that funny twitch in his face when you talk to him. It bothers me."

"He has facial ticks, sometimes. But it's never affected his job performance."

"Do it!" Finley rose from his metal chair so fast that it banged against the trailer wall. "Do it or I'll ask Roland to hire another foreman. There are plenty of unemployed men in this area looking for jobs. You're nothing special."

Paul held his breath. The last thing he needed was to get laid off. The money he was pulling in helped cover most of his father's medical expenses. North Carolina opted out of the National Health Care Plan, meaning everyone living there had to fend for themselves.

Finley exited the trailer, flicking the toothpick into the metal basket by the door as an exclamation of his authority.

Later that day Paul gathered his crew together.

"Finley needs you guys to work through the holiday."

"What?"

"Man, no way."

"Yes, that's about how I told him. Listen, I know you guys don't like him, and to be frank, I'm not a big fan of the man either. But he promised that if we do this, we can add those days to Christmas. You're all a great bunch of guys, and I know you're working your tails off as it is."

"Is Finley working then?" asked Pete.

"I doubt it," Tom replied. "He'll be filling that fat gut of his with so much stuffing he'll be shitting bread bricks."

The others laughed.

"I'm not sure," Paul answered. "But if he's not, I plan on bringing in a couple of turkeys for us all. No need to go without a good meal."

"You're a good guy, Paul."

"Thanks, men. I'm sorry to have to tell you this."

The workers slowly dispersed and individually patted Paul on the shoulder on the way back to their zones. Stan was the last one in line.

"Stan, I need to talk to you for a moment." Paul put his arm on Stan's shoulder and walked him over to a stack of lumber.

"This is completely not right, and I'm going to find a way to bring you back—" Paul paused when he noticed Stan's face twitch with apprehension. "But...I have to let you go."

Stan was a quiet man. More like a listener. A very good listener. He knew his job well and what was expected of him. All anyone had to do was point to a blueprint and give a few instructions, and he was on his way. No questions asked. Except this time.

"Why, Paul? What did I do wrong?"

"Nothing wrong. Nothing at all." It broke Paul inside to know the real reason. "It's just that Finley says I'm overstaffed. But I mean it. I'm going to try to get you back." Paul kept his hand on Stan's shoulder and held firm.

"I understand." Stan smiled back as much as one can smile when given such bad news.

"You can finish up the day. And I mean what I say." Paul removed his hand and reached out his right to shake. Stan shook back, then turned and walked over to a stack of two-by-six wall studs. Paul remained frozen in place.

Thanksgiving came and passed. Finley showed up Thanksgiving morning and stayed long enough to prod the men and upset Paul's charitable offerings. They had one hour to consume the turkey and fixings he brought, then it was back to raising frames. The men grew increasingly frustrated.

Back home, Paul's father wasn't faring well with new medication prescribed for his ALS. After receiving well over one hundred million dollars during the 2014 "ice-bucket challenge," the ALS medical community still hadn't found an effective cure for the debilitating disease. Such was the power of social media—it could raise a lot of money and awareness for a cause, but no one really knew how well that money was spent. New drugs only helped to slow the progression.

Paul could see the toll it was taking on his dad's spirit. Paul Sr. was always an independent man. Now something as simple as watering the garden or fixing dinner proved to be a challenge. His wife, Paul's mother, had passed away three years earlier of a stroke. A caregiver came to the house just two days a week, but she'd mostly just tidy up the place and take out the trash. A physical therapist would cost more.

So Paul kept his mouth shut.

Blustery winds kicked in the second week of December and never let up. Global warming had altered the warm serenity of the South. The summers were scalding and the winters were frigid. Mild was rarely a term used to describe the weather.

Paul and his men worked extra hard to get the time off for Christmas. But the job site was like a tundra, making it difficult to move and breathe. Dirt cracked underfoot. Tire tracks formed when the temperature was above freezing were like fossil prints. A boot toe would occasionally get caught in a groove and send a worker tumbling over. The cold was even worse three stories up. Six of the ten buildings were framed and ready for siding. But it was slow going. Finley insisted that all ten be framed by New Year's.

"Paul," Finley gloated with his legs propped up on his metal desk, "you and your men will have to work through the Christmas holiday."

"No Finley, I told my men they can have it off, and they'll have it off."

"Do you want me to go to Roland and tell them this? How you were behind in foundations and now you'll be behind in framing?"

"The only reason we're behind is because you took Tom and Pete off foundation. Christmas is just five days away, for god's sake. Many of the guys have made travel plans to see their families. You can't do this."

"I *can* do this, and I *will* do this. I don't know how you pussies did things up in Seattle, but you're in the South now."

"You know what, Finley? My father is ill. He can barely move around. He may not be with us in a year or so. So I'd like to spend Christmas day with my dad."

"So bring him here. He can watch you work." Finley seemed stoked by his crass comeback. Paul looked back in disbelief. The man was heartless, after all.

"Time's a-wastin'," Finley continued. "Tell them they can have more time off for New Year's." He chuckled and exited the trailer like a stoked Grinch retreating from a toyless home.

Paul pondered a way to tell his crew.

Light snow trickled down from the sky on Christmas Eve and early Christmas Day. It gathered on the tops of wood joists and crossbeams in soft, billowy piles. Nail guns echoed in the cold air like machine guns slowed to half speed. At one point Paul pulled his truck around to building eight and tuned the radio to a holiday music station.

All twenty-two men labored through the chilling winds, which picked up Christmas morning. By noon a foot of snow had fallen. By two it was two feet. Tiny shards of ice flicked into raw skin as near-blizzard conditions put a halt to the work. The men gathered around the trailer where Paul had coffee and hot chocolate waiting.

"Guys, this is just crazy. The roads are gonna get congested soon. And working right now is too treacherous. I want you to go home to your families before conditions get much worse. I'll handle Finley, don't you worry."

"I'd like to handle him right now, that fat bastard." Pete had to cancel his trip to South Carolina where his daughter and new son-in-law had invited him for the day.

"Yeah, I bet he's sitting pretty in a nice warm house inhaling ham slices and cranberry sauce. I hope he chokes on it," Tom interjected.

Paul waited for all the men to leave before locking up the trailer and wiping the snow off his truck. He had promised his father he'd be home Christmas evening. It was already four o'clock when he left the work site. By then large swells of snow had formed on the country roads like motionless waves. Some of the crests rose up to his front bumper. By five it was a whiteout. At times he wasn't sure if he was still driving on the road or about to enter a ditch. He finally had to pull over and wait it out.

At seven o'clock a large plow passed along the side of his truck and removed much of the snow in his path. After shoveling around his front wheels, he was able to maneuver his truck back onto the road and cautiously navigate the icy side streets. A revolving red light reflected off the moonlit snow as he approached his father's home. There was an ambulance parked at the curb.

Paul rushed inside where the caretaker, Jolene, was crying at the front entrance. His father had fallen down the stairs and broken his neck. He was pronounced dead minutes before Paul arrived. Near his body was a paper-mache star half coated in gold glitter. It was something Paul had made as a child and his father had kept in storage all these years. He was on his way to putting it on the Christmas tree when his legs froze up and he fell. It was to be a surprise.

Had Paul been home earlier he could have helped his dad, who would then still be alive. Finley's suggestion ripped through Paul's mind like a razor blade. That cold, insensitive man would pay. Paul filled out the World Order Alliance "People Reduction" form online. Two days later they approved his immediate request with a simple text message.

"Do it."

Finley returned to the construction site the day before New Year's Eve to assess the progress. All ten buildings were framed, and siding had been started on the first. That didn't stop him from calling Paul aside again. But this time Paul and his men had a plan.

"I expected half the buildings to be fully sided by now. You'll have to work through New Year's."

"We already plan to, Finley." Paul rubbed his cold hands together.

"You'll never do it." Finley laughed. "And when you don't, I'll be making that call into Roland to get your replacement."

"Don't you worry. Hey, the guys and I chipped in and bought you a bottle of your favorite, Fireball Cinnamon Whiskey." Paul pulled a bottle of the potent liquor from his bottom desk drawer along with two highball glasses. "How about we settle this like adults?"

"What do you mean?"

"Drink me under the table."

"Ha ha, you'll lose."

"If I lose, you can put that call into Roland. If I win, you'll get off my back and let me do my job."

"You're half my size. There's no way you can take me on this."

"So let's start." Paul opened the bottle and poured both glasses to half height. Finley bumbled over to Paul's desk, grabbed his glass, and downed the whiskey in less than two seconds. He puckered his fat lips and exposed his big teeth.

"Oh yeah, that's good stuff."

Paul drank his a bit more slowly. Then he refilled both glasses.

"A toast, to a terrific New Year coming." Paul raised his up.

"For me, yes. For you...I'd get those resumes out." Finley slightly lifted his glass without touching Paul's.

Ten minutes went by before the alcohol began to hit both

men. Finley's eyes warmed like a baby suckling a pacifier. Paul's raged with an inner fire.

"Oof. It's hot in here. How about we take this outside? I can check on my men."

"I can think of nothing better than to watch you lose in front of your crew."

The two exited the trailer into the brisk afternoon air. Tom and Pete and the other men looked down from their lofty positions while Paul and Finley strolled by underfoot. The two drinkers leaned against a stack of plywood. Paul rested the bottle of Fireball on top of the pile after pouring each another glass.

"Men," Finley shouted, "let this be a lesson to you all. Your boss, Paul-ee here, has challenged me to a drinking contest." Finley paused to burp. "Never challenge a fat man to a drinking contest. You'll lose every time." Finley swigged the liquor quickly and rapped his glass down for another.

For the rest of the bottle, Paul put his lips up to his glass, but dumped the contents around the corner of the stack when Finley wasn't looking. It was easy to do, since Finley began closing his eyes with every new shot. And Paul knew why. Alcohol may not topple the bastard in the drunken sense, but it always put him to sleep. He had witnessed it several times in the trailer since he took on the project. He would smell the whiskey on the man's breath in the early morning, then walk in hours later to find Finley slouched in his chair like an inebriated seal. And now he was about to get harpooned.

Half an hour later the ricochet of nail guns and the roar of heavy machinery came to an abrupt halt. All the workers scrambled down the scaffolding like ants to a sugar pile. Finley was flat on his ass in the crusty snow. The men surrounded him while Tom hurried over to the nearby crane.

"Hey fat oaf!" Pete shouted. Finley didn't respond. His snoring was so loud that it resonated over the start of the crane's engine. Tom rolled the machine to within a few yards of the stack. The sixty-foot boom swiveled around until it was directly above Finley's resting body. Tom lowered the hoist line to Paul and the others, who immediately secured it around Finley's waist and crotch with a nylon strap. It took three men to roll him into it. Once the harness was in place, Paul gave Tom the thumbs up. Finley's body slowly lifted into the air until he hung nearly fifty feet from the ground. His head rested on his shoulder while he continued to snore away. Tom locked the hoist in place and joined the men. They cheerfully and laughingly gazed up to their former project supervisor before departing the site for the holiday weekend.

"High, but not so mighty anymore." Paul gloated.

A Nor'easter swept into the lower South that night and New Year's Eve. Finley awoke in the darkness and wailed for hours before the heavy sleet came in. By midday his body was coated from head to toe with a thick, wet slush. It would begin to freeze just hours before nightfall. He shook and shivered until he could no longer move. Then icicles formed at the tips of his fingers, the tips of his boots, and the tip of his nose. His bare white skin crystallized into a silvery glitter. As the calendar year turned over to 2022, a dead Finley Ross dangled in the moonlight like a giant sky ornament. His face was frozen in place with a haunting upward stare, like Jack Nicholson at the end of *The Shining*. There would be no more shouting.

A week later Paul was promoted to project supervisor. Tom became crew foreman. And Stan was hired back to work. By then they had lowered Finley's body onto the ground where the empty bottle of Fireball laid by his side. Authorities assumed he had drank himself to death in celebration of the New Year and passed out in the cold. The crew finished all ten buildings by mid-May and received generous bonuses.

****

Let this be a lesson to you parents out there. When your child acts out and you do nothing, you are opening the door for another monster in our world. But you can stop the cycle with a well-placed hand, a steadfast and authoritative attitude, and unwavering perseverance. And in Finley's case, perhaps, three simple words:

"Eat your broccoli."

Litterbugs

A plastic grocery bag, a plastic straw, a plastic lid, and a plastic cup. A Minute Maid can, a Budweiser beer bottle, a Slurpee tumbler, a Trident gum wrapper, a business card from Tim's Auto Repair, and a CareOne brand anti-diarrhea pillbox. A deflated red balloon, a condom, a tampon, a rubber glove, a spark plug, foam wrap, and a used ketchup packet. A Grizzly wintergreen skoal tin, a Cheetos bag, an Utz bag, a Doritos bag, and a 7-Eleven pizza slice box. More beer bottles, more food wrappers, more cups, hundreds of cigarette butts, and enough plastic bottles that when placed end to end they would exceed the one-hundred-foot stretch of highway in which all the other items were found.

Stew Henderson waded into the shallow ditch along Route 23 to retrieve another plastic lid floating on the water surface. This was the third time he was assigned to this section of road in the past three months. With each pass he had left it in pristine condition. So clean and beautiful that one could almost view the adjacent field as an immaculate entrance to the tranquil woods just fifty feet away. Like an unspoiled nature preserve.

But this time he found more hazardous refuse: two half-empty paint cans, an antifreeze container, and unlabeled spray bottles with God-knows-what chemicals inside. It made him sick. He thought about how all these items ended up here. He knew from an online study that eighty percent of all litter is intentionally left behind. The other twenty percent escapes from truck beds and open car windows. Certainly these items were too big to be sucked out of a passing vehicle. No, someone threw them here with complete disregard for how they could upset the environment.

It was the beauty of the natural world that got Stew involved with the Saginaw highway cleanup department. He lived just ten miles away along the Cass River in a small bungalow he had renovated with the money he earned from collecting trash. It was a terrific location. His backyard disappeared into a ten-acre section of woods where he'd often escape on the weekends or on his days off. It was like an oasis. Bright green mosses carpeted the forest floor and continued up the tree bases. Ferns unfurled into large patches that extended for yards in every direction. Wildflowers popped up in unexpected locations, like the patch of Lady's Slippers he discovered the previous week. Mushrooms and other fungi sporadically appeared like surprise alien growth. Some were bright red. Others a deep, lush orange. And the creatures—the insects, the birds, the snakes, the squirrels and everything that flew and crawled and jumped and dug and sang in this untouched sanctuary—it was all so perfect. Oh how he wished the whole world could be like this. He had so much compassion for nature, in part from the hours of TV documentaries he had watched as a kid. But it was also something he noticed more once he got older. You come to appreciate what may be gone someday.

It was sad and frustrating to see how the area where he worked had been mistreated again. He poked and stabbed the remaining debris as if each thrust of his trash stick somehow magically did away with the person responsible. Another cigarette pack, a drugstore receipt, a foam cup, an empty pasta box, and a McDonald's Big Mac carton. He'd seen a lot of those today. This one rested just at the edge of the ditch. It was the last item. In defiance, he raised his stick high in the air before slamming it into the carton like a dagger into a rock. But this time it made an unusual squishy sound. *Maybe part of the burger was still inside?* When he pulled the stick up to inspect it, he was horrified by what he saw. A frog had made its way inside the box, and he had stabbed it to death. Its legs twitched for a few moments before going limp. Then a portion of its insides flowed out of its tiny body where the sharp point of the stick had penetrated through. There was no chance it would survive.

Stew was devastated.

Back at his bungalow that night, in the room where he kept his vivariums, Stew flipped through his field guidebooks to identify the frog's species. He had gently placed the creature into another box and brought it home with him. He owned several reptiles and amphibians, which he meticulously researched to create the optimum environments in which they could thrive. Four large glass terrariums lined the walls, each an authentic recreation of a natural habitat. In one, a pair of brilliant green day geckos with crimson spots along their bodies nestled inside a three-foot-high enclosure. Live plants, bamboo shoots, and rolled bark provided plenty of places to climb and roost. In the second, a twenty-gallon tank, a two-foot ball python curled around its water bowl. When it wasn't resting, a vertical maze of branches and hollowed logs gave the docile creature room to explore and hide. In the third tank, a pack of brown armadillo lizards blended into a desert landscape, complete with cave hideaways and native cacti and succulents. And in the last, a dozen golden poison dart frogs (Phyllobates terribilis) cohabited another tropical enclosure. This tank was outfitted with an automatic mister and a realistic waterfall.

He opened up the box and examined the dead frog, still

heartbroken over what had happened. It was a northern cricket frog, commonly found along the banks of shallow streams. It must have made its way to the ditch from the nearby woods after the recent heavy rainfall. Its face stared back at him with a grotesque, forlorn look, as if it were sending a signal that something needed to be done. It could not die in vain.

Stew placed a dandelion from the front yard on top of the frog's body, then sealed the box shut. After dinner, he buried the creature in the backyard under the maple tree where his dog Scooter was laid to rest two years earlier. As he stood up and wiped his eyes, a gust of wind blew a stray piece of paper to his feet.

"Dear God," he sighed.

He reached down and picked it up. It was a flyer for the Saginaw Fair, which began in two weeks. "Bring Your Whole Family. Loads of FUN!" it read.

"Yeah, I'll bet." He wadded the unwelcome advertisement into a tiny ball and tossed it into his garage recycle bin before calling it a night.

The next day Stew visited the local PetValue for supplies. It was situated in the middle of a long strip mall burgeoning with an array of shops: an Italian eatery, a nail salon, a hardware store, a pizza shop, a vision center, and a large grocery chain. The parking lot bustled with shoppers. As he exited the pet store, he noticed a little boy, probably no more than four years old, trailing several feet behind his mother. The kid had a toy squirt gun in his hand still inside the packaging, of which he pulled and tore at with all his might. After freeing the gun, he let the hard plastic wrapper fall to the ground and continued on.

"Miss," Stew spoke out. "Miss?" The woman turned around. "I think your son dropped something."

The woman sent Stew a stone stare, then waited for her son to catch up. She briefly looked over at the litter, then back at Stew, and rolled her eyes. It was clear it didn't matter to her. Someone who worked there would probably pick it up. Not her problem.

Over near the grocery store a woman with a crying baby pushed her shopping cart to the side of the entrance and began changing the child's diaper. Stew entered his car and watched from his window. After she was done, she picked up the baby and her two bags, but left the soiled diaper in the seat of the cart. She walked away thinking nothing of it.

"Disgusting!" Stew groaned.

In front of the pizza shop, two teenagers leaned against the outside window while eating slices and smoking cigarettes. Their bottles of Pepsi rested on the ledge. After they finished, they tossed the empty cartons into a nearby overflowing receptacle where they immediately tumbled to the ground. They left their cups behind.

And outside the hardware store, a man opened up a small bag of items—probably screws, or picture hangers, or some other do-hickies— sending the receipt and sales flyer to the wind.

It was now clear to Stew how things ended up where they did. Obliviousness. Sheer disregard. An uncaring, unencumbered, self-indulgent, aloof attitude that permeated most of modern society. He had seen it get worse through the years. Thank God there were at least stringent standards on things like air quality and emissions. But there was little check on people themselves. A few cities, like Washington, D.C. back in 2014, had implemented strict fines for littering. But again, it was all about enforcing the laws. He saw no cops in this parking lot today. You can't fine someone unless you catch him or her in the act. And would a fine be enough anyway?

No.

Stew pulled out of the lot and headed south on Interstate 75. As he crossed over Dixie Highway, a dark shadow flew in front of him like a giant prehistoric bird. The harsh stutter of propellers arrived a second later. It was a helicopter heading west. Once it reached altitude, it unleashed a giant banner tethered to a thin transparent line: "108th Annual Saginaw Fair * August 7-15." The copter circled over the highway several times before heading back toward the city.

While Stew bemoaned the notion of hordes of people gathered together to create one giant mess, an idea snapped into his head like a lost memory. It was the perfect solution. A plan like no other. Righteously vengeful and inventive to boot. It was as if all the pieces had been put in front of him. But he'd have to work quickly.

A dastardly smile washed over his face as he envisioned the details of execution.

That weekend Stew retrieved from storage the small drone he had purchased at the City Hobby Shop some years ago. Back when drones were all the rage in 2016, it became the must-buy item on everyone's Christmas list. Youtube and other social media sites were subsequently flooded with videos of amateur aerial footage. The best clips were when the flying devices took a spill, or the one where a ram chased down a rogue drone and head-butted it to the ground. But some captured astounding footage of parks and other natural settings. Like most fads, though, the novelty soon wore off. Hobbyists retired their outdated aerial machines for newer electronic toys.

Stew had purchased the Vango II model, which came equipped with a built-in camera and a remote video monitor. The receiver also had a digital radar so he could see exactly where the drone was at any time. The ten-inch-wide flyer could navigate through the most congested settings with little effort. He dusted off the device, then charged up the battery pack. On a full load it could last for several hours. Then he took it to his backyard and set it free. He circled the drone overhead a few times before directing it toward the back woods.

For the first time he viewed his private refuge the way a bird might see it. No, more like a dragonfly. He hovered over the fern gullies, then zigzagged throughout the trees like an acrobatic pilot in some futuristic movie. He guided the flyer along the small creek that traversed the northern border and barely skimmed the water surface. At one point the drone was approached by a curious hummingbird. The on-board camera sent back stunning images, which he recorded onto an internal memory card. It's no wonder he hadn't thought of doing this before. After a few close encounters with low-hanging branches and tall brush, he was able to navigate the drone throughout most of the ten acres without incident.

He would practice every night the following week.

On the Monday before the fair, after another long day picking up more stray rubbish from filthy locals, Stew tackled the next phase of his plan. He visited the hobby shop, oddly still in business, and purchased a small can of bright red paint and white adhesive lettering. Then he hit up a toy store on the other side of town. He had seen the item he wanted advertised on TV a month back. As he walked up and down the aisles, he was amazed by how advanced toys were these days. Everything was electronic. And everything seemed to have a corresponding computer app to go with it. If only they'd made this stuff when he was a kid.

On the end of aisle three, next to Tank Master and Gorilla Ninja, was the accessory he was looking for. For kids 8 and up, it read. It was perfect: small and lightweight, and even came with its own separate remote. He'd have to alter it a bit for his purposes, but that would be the fun part. He'd start work on it tonight.

Later that evening, Stew unscrewed the cap to the red paint and delivered long, thick strokes onto the body of the Vango drone. He'd want to coat everything but the propellers, which he removed beforehand. He could have just taped it off and spray-painted the thing, but there was something enjoyable about taking the time to do it the old way. It was like working on his model airplanes, something he hadn't done in years. A long shelf in his den served as a permanent display for his creations: a Boeing B-17 Flying Fortress, a F4U4 Corsair Fighter, a B-25 Mitchell Bomber, and a P-40 Tiger Shark. Plus with each stroke he could think about his plan more and imagine how it might all go down.

"There." Stew placed the newly painted drone on some old newspapers next to a fan. He'd wait till tomorrow to apply the lettering. Then the attachment. He'd want the rest of the week to practice again. Only five days to the fair, and they were expecting a sizable crowd this year.

The more, the better.

The night before the fair's opening day, which was expected to attract the most attendees due to the exquisite lineup of B-list country singers and the all-enticing trucker mud runs, Stew finalized his preparations. He printed out a map of the fair to identify the precise locations of the vendors, the rides, and the exits. It had been two years since he'd attended, mostly to listen to the off-color jabs the jester would hurl before getting dunked in the water by angry ball throwers. The layout remained pretty much the same. The two or three cops on duty tended to hang out by the entrance. By midday they'd be half hammered. By nightfall they'd be over by the trucker pavilion where most of the bad boy fights erupted. It would be a great diversion for what was going on elsewhere.

In the wee hours of the morning, Stew slipped on a pair of elastic gloves and delicately completed phase three. It was much easier than he thought. And so very little was needed. He chuckled over the irony of it all. Unlike the rampage of an angry teen who'd endured years of bullying, Stew's was a noble cause. Plus, it was nothing personal, really. And everyone had a choice. They'd be sufficiently forewarned. Even the World Order Alliance agreed. They approved his application in just one day.

"You're right on target!" they exclaimed in their email.

The line to the ticket booth wrapped three-quarters the way around the parking lot an hour before the gates were to open. Seats for the evening concert and the mud run were an extra five dollars each. Gone were the days of one price for all admissions. It was the morning of Saturday, August 7, 2021, and it looked as though it would be a terrific day—weather-wise.

Stew stood in line with the others and quietly observed. There were the mom gangs with their restless broods of brats. Kids so pent-up with energy they'd circle around their parents like the rides they hoped to be on soon. Then there were the dads, not awake enough at nine o'clock in the morning to give a damn. Their time would come when the sun went down and the beer tents lit up. Teens tended to sleep in on Saturday, but a few anxiously waited in line. They'd be in and out of the fair all day long with their stamped hands. Stew intended to leave at one point, too. But he'd still be there, metaphorically.

Once inside, he scoped out the premises to make sure he hadn't missed anything. The giant Ferris wheel was at the far end like the years before. Some of the ride placements were so predictable. It was as if the setup crew used dead spots in the grass to position them. There were a few new attractions: the Swirley Whirler (an obvious promotion for the new animated movie, *Swirley*), and a mini roller coaster for kids named The Looper. Most of the food vendors returned, including Don's Donut Burger. That was always a hit. And so was the litter from it. Sticky paper wrappers left behind everywhere, as Stew recalled. One adhered to the heel of his shoe last time.

By noon the place had roared to life. Wheels whirled, scramblers scrambled, and plungers plunged. There was already a puke spot in front of the Rocky Roller. Moms tossed back large cups of diet soda and chewed on the ice. Their kids waved and shouted from the confines of metal chairs. Dads snapped photos with their newfangled cameras, hoping for impressive shots with raised arms and elated faces. The 2021 Saginaw Fair was in full swing.

Stew downed a Coke and leaned against one of the trash receptacles. There were twelve throughout the grounds—one every thirty feet or so. You couldn't miss them. But by one o'clock it was apparent that some people already had. Straw wrappers, cotton candy cones, cigarette butts, and spent ride tickets popped up everywhere. Then there were the colored slips of paper from the retail vendors inside the commercial barns. Most advertised roofing products and heated hot tubs. Most didn't make it to the trash can outside the door, either. Instead, they blew all over everywhere. Stew wished he had his stabbing stick.

After devouring a smoked turkey leg—even vigilantes need to eat—Stew walked over to the main restroom. The inside trash bin overflowed with paper hand wipes. One of the stall toilets was already plugged, and unflushed. *Gross.* And the urinal he waited in line for had wads of chewed gum stuck to the splatter guard. His rage was quickly building. It was time to send out the warning signals.

He had parked his car behind the strip mall that backed up to woods behind the fairgrounds. That way he was close, but obscured. This would be his operation center. Inside he had rigged his drone receiver to a larger monitor, which rested on the passenger seat. He placed a note pad with a pen on the divider. All he had to do was double-check the drone for battery strength, then set it loose. It registered in the far green. *Excellent.*

Stew unrolled his car window and looked around to see if anyone was standing nearby. No one. The mall was home to non-essential businesses—a dental office and a design firm—usually closed on the weekends. He balanced the small drone on his hand, held it outside, then raised the lever on the controller. The drone instantly lifted ten feet above his car hood. He tested out the rotation, turning the drone a full 360. His video monitor confirmed the maneuver. It was ready to go.

Stew chuckled like a demented clown while he navigated the flyer over the grove of trees and approached the joyous spectacle.

Children giggled and pointed as the bright red drone nestled in among the crowd. The parents thought it was some vendor promoting a new toy. Authorities paid no attention at all, surprisingly. They were too busy orchestrating setup for the evening attractions. The white lettering on the side of the drone was unmistakable: "PLEASE DON'T LITTER."

Stew swiftly guided the flyer above the fairgoers, just enough out of reach so it couldn't be swatted down. When it came to a trash receptacle, the drone would hover above it like a glaring beacon. After a minute or two it would continue to the next can. And so on. Stew circled the device over the main drag several times to give onlookers sufficient warning. One teen purposely flicked his cigarette butt at it. Stew raised the drone a bit higher, put it in hover mode, then jotted down the kid's description.

"Dude with Yosemite Sam tattoo."

In front of the Ferris wheel, a woman in a pink shirt and tight jeans dropped a half-eaten snow cone to the ground. Stew took note.

"Bimbo in pink pullover."

This went on for the next two hours. By four o'clock the list was thirty people long:

Fat man in Carhartts
Chick with nose ring
Teen with U of M T-shirt
Woman with twin stroller
Dude with mutton chops
Girl with long red hair
Superman shirt guy

And so on. Any kid who appeared prepubescent was excluded. They were, perhaps, too young to know better. Hopefully they'd learn from this.

Operation Litterbug began at precisely five o'clock. By then a few of the offenders were making their way to their cars. He'd have to catch them before they drove off.

Stew raced the drone over the entrance, then settled it close behind the mutton chop dude. The guy was walking alone with car keys in hand. He turned around when he heard the hum of the pursuing flyer.

"What? Get this the fuck out of here."

The man looked around to see if he could spot the controller. He jumped up to grab the thing, but Stew was quick to raise it. The man turned around and continued to walk. The drone closely followed. Just as he was about to confront it again, Stew grabbed the plastic remote and pressed the red fire button. The man swatted the back of his neck as if an insect had just bitten him. Stew circled the drone around to view his face. Dude was just three steps from his car when his eyes began to roll in their sockets. Next, his legs buckled at the knees. He fell onto the grass in between his car and the next. His body twitched for a few seconds, then went limp. It was that fast.

The second victim was the woman with the twin stroller. She had just placed her toddlers into their rear car seats when the needle penetrated the skin on her left hand. She collapsed thirty seconds later. Her body slumped over the steering wheel with her driver's door still wide open.

Stew navigated the drone back to the fairgrounds. No one would suspect anything at this point. The parking lot was far enough away and the two bodies were obscured from direct view. But he'd have to work quickly with the next round.

By six o'clock the lead-up music for the concert permeated the fair atmosphere. On top of that was the ruckus of the ride jingles. The uneven measure of the carousel tune was most nauseating. The older men gravitated to the beer tents where a host of adult games were in session. Sexy Shooter entailed firing pellets at scantly clad cardboard cutouts. Stew spotted the fat man in Carhartts laughing off to the side. Every time the man swigged his Blue Moon, the foam ran over the rim and down his hand. This guy was a slob through and through.

The chick with the nose ring was getting a temporary tattoo at Thelma's Tats. A purple dragon with a magic wand was the one she chose. No surprise there, Stew thought.

The teen with the University of Michigan shirt attempted to dunk the heckler with his fast pitch. "They call it maize, we call it corn!" The performer jeered the school's maize and blue coloring with the well-known catchphrase. The third ball hit spot center. The jester went down. And so would the teen, in a few.

Stew maneuvered the drone's watchful eye right up to dusk. By then some of the people had settled in to enjoy the nighttime shows. Over at the truck run, men in boots hosed down piles of dirt until the course was thick and soupy. The drivers lined up their vehicles and revved their engines. One of them was the teen with the Yosemite Sam tat.

At seven the first country performer, a Carrie Underwood clone, took to the raised stage and hollered to the packed house.

"How y'all doin' tonight here in Saginaaaw!"

The crowd roared.

Over at the trucker pavilion, the first entrant raced around the corner and got stuck in the muck just ten feet in. A tow line had to be attached to his grill to pull him out.

Within the concession stands, the woman in pink who dropped the snow cone bit down on a large soft pretzel. Stew angled the drone from five feet away and shot the needle in her forehead. She limped to an unlit picnic table and keeled over.

The toxin he had swabbed off the backs of the poison dart frogs the previous night was as powerful as he had read. One milligram could take down two African bull elephants, according to Wikipedia. The indigenous Choco Emberá tribe of the Colombian rainforest still coated the tips of blow darts with it for killing game. Stew used the minuscule needles of the Stinging Nettle plant as the means of delivery. The herbaceous perennial was abundant along the Michigan highways. He picked off the delicate needles with tweezers and let them dry out before dipping them in the fluid. The toy gun he had purchased, the Popper, came loaded with harmless plastic pellets. He narrowed the cylinder with a cocktail straw to accommodate the pin-sized darts.

Once the neurotoxin reached the bloodstream, muscle paralysis was assured. Limbs would go limp, breathing would subside, and the muscles around the heart would fail. Death was quick. Normally captive dart frogs lose their toxicity. But Stew kept the creatures on a steady diet of native South American ants and beetles in which it acquired the poison. It was all so easy, and ironic. It was the accidental killing of a frog that provoked him into action. Now it was the frogs getting revenge.

As sunset illuminated the fairgrounds with a golden hue, Stew set his plan into full gear. First he took out the Superman shirt guy, who was just about to enter the restroom when a needle pierced his left calf. He collapsed inside the rank stall. The man in the Carhartts took a needle to the eye while flirting with the redhead. She thought he had passed out from drinking. The next shot bit into her exposed cleavage. She tumbled on top of him. And when the teen with the Yosemite Sam tattoo tore through the mud, Stew zipped the drone alongside and shot him in the cheek. The crowd watched the kid stagger out of his vehicle and fall face first into the muck. Everyone gasped.

Fritters flung, drumsticks dropped, and onion blossoms peeled. In essence, all shit broke loose. People bolted for the exit gates. Most were too inebriated to know which way to turn. Some knocked over the full trash cans, sending more litter underfoot.

They had to be darted as well. Even in chaos Stew demanded decorum. Within five minutes all the people on his list, plus another six, were dead. The litterers had become litter themselves. Before the cops caught on, Stew lifted the drone straight up into the darkened sky. It sped away like an alien saucer.

"Massacre at the Saginaw Fair" was the news headline the following day. No one saw the drone come in direct contact with any of the victims, so it was assumed that something else was responsible. A serial killer who set out to poison the masses through food and drink, perhaps? The needles were so tiny and deep under the skin that they were undetectable at the autopsies. And the toxicology reports, as the public knew through years of television forensics, would take weeks.

In that time Stew drove throughout the state and scoured more public settings for violators. A death here, a death there. One less litterbug here, one less litterbug there. It was all quite enjoyable. And the streets looked a lot cleaner.

In the peaceful woods behind his home the following spring, and along the many highways and byways, birds flew from tree to tree with a little less fear. Insects had a greater abundance of flowering plants to pollinate. Critters had more places to hide and food to eat. And at night, when the moonlight bathed the forest floors in a phosphorescent glow, young frogs sang their mating calls with a bit more gusto.

They knew they were protected.

Terror Garden

This year the theme was color, and seventy-two-year-old Agnes Woodward proved, once again, that she knew just the right plants to cultivate at just the right time to put on a good show. Tall purple irises lined the walkway up to her front door, where large pink peonies adorned both sides of the entrance. Along the brick front, beds of yellow daylilies mixed with blue salvia and snow-white lily of the valley. Bushes of red hibiscus mingled in the front yard with eye-popping orange dahlias. And above, dish-plate-sized white magnolia blooms unfurled against dark green leaves like giant floating orbs.

Her backyard was equally impressive. Pathways of perennials and annuals in all colors curved around ornate stone sculptures of mischievous cherubs and mythical gods. In the center, a cascading waterfall supplied frothy fresh water to a pool of giant orange, white, and black-speckled coy. Even the shady spots under the old oak tree in the far corner bursted with color. Within the variegated hostas were the brilliant purple, lime, maroon, yellow, and pink leaves of various coleus varieties. A few of the hybrids Agnes created herself.

The four women and one man, whose gardens preceded, shuffled daintily along the walkways. Their heads swiveled left to right like health inspectors in a restaurant kitchen. They smiled and nodded as Agnes pointed out the various specimens. All had the same thing on their minds: this old lady has outdone us again. It was the eighth annual neighborhood garden tour in Lake Jackson, Virginia. And for the fifth year in a row it was obvious who would take home the prize.

"She couldn't have done all this herself," they'd whisper. And they were right. Her husband, the tanned and spry sixty-five-year-old Albert Woodward, had done much of the heavy work. But it was Agnes who spent hours online and inside her test greenhouse to create the incredible display.

Albert exited the back door with a tray of cold beverages. All heads instantly shifted toward him. This was the real reward, they thought. Albert was one of those playboy types, like a movie star who barely aged. His jet-black hair had only minor streaks of gray running through it, and it was all there. His muscled chest pushed against the tight, stretchy fabric of his blue pullover shirt, and his immense thighs bulged under his tan-colored shorts as if they'd tear through the seams. His ocean-blue eyes and seductive smile could make even the coldest person swoon.

"Drinks?"

"Thank you!" the visitors said in unison as their hands reached out and bumped into one another.

"Thank you, darling." Albert lowered his body and tilted his head so his wife could plant a soft kiss on his cheek. "Everyone, you know Albert?"

Five heads with beaming smiles simultaneously nodded.

"I want to thank Albert for the tireless work he put into the garden again this year."

"Oh baby, it's all your doing." Albert draped his sinewy arm around his wife's shoulder and pulled her close. Then he pecked her cheek and quickly disappeared back into the house. The visitors quietly sighed. It was the last they'd see of him.

"You've done a marvelous job, Agnes."

"Yes," the others agreed.

"Where do you buy most of your plants?" one asked. "Merrifield?"

"Oh no," Agnes responded. "They charge *way* too much. I either create my own hybrids, or purchase them on discount at Home Depot."

"I see, that's very impressive."

"You're all welcome to some. I've potted up a batch for each of you to take home."

It was customary at the end of the garden tour for neighbors to engage in a plant exchange. However, it was Agnes who always went out of her way to pot up the most promising specimens. Others simply tossed their weakest plants into cracked pots with worn-out soil. Plants that were probably meant for the compost bin. But not Agnes. She genuinely cared about the people around her, and it showed in how she treated them. This year she gave out vibrant coleus cuttings along with pots brimming with a wonderful silver grass.

"Put these two together and you'll have a fabulous display."

After the tour, fifty-two-year-old Patricia Livingston, who lived next door, reluctantly handed Agnes the $100 gift certificate to Terragotta, an online garden accessory store. It was everyone's favorite place to shop for unique items. And their prices were decent.

"Thank you so much. I'm going to put this to good use. I can't wait to plan out for next year."

Agnes mingled with her guests for the next few minutes, all the while hearing her name repeatedly whispered under envious breaths. She knew why they really came—to see her husband. They'd always ask how Albert was doing when they caught her working alone in the front yard. She also knew that some of them had done some pretty bad things over the years. Things that they thought she'd never find out. But Agnes was well aware of what went on around her. Secrets traveled throughout the neighborhood like dandelion seeds on a windy day. It was painful to realize that those she did her best to befriend could be so malicious.

But what hurt her most was how they treated her after Albert died.

She had just finished preparing dinner—Albert's favorite, oven-fried chicken—when she heard a loud crash coming from the back porch.

"Albert, is that you?" she said before drying her hands with a kitchen towel and opening the screen door. At the base of the steps were large and small chips from clay pots that led like a trail to where her husband lay on his side. Agnes rushed to Albert just as he rolled over and looked up at her with his frightened blue eyes. His hands were clutching his chest.

"Oh, dear Albert," she said while holding onto his shoulder. "I need to get help." She was about to go back inside for the phone when Albert whispered for her to stay with him.

"I want to thank you for making me the happiest man," he said. "You always took care of me, even when I went astray. You are a very special woman. You're my apple dumpling."

Agnes sat down at her husband's side and caressed his thick black hair while he peacefully passed away. It was as if he had just fallen asleep, like the many times next to her on the couch after watching a long movie together. Or when they were younger and stayed out late after sunset on the Maryland beaches. Just like that. Within two hours the ambulance came and took Albert away from her, and Agnes sat at the dinner table alone. In front of her was a spread of food prepared with the same care she put into her garden—oven-fried chicken breasts marinated in buttermilk and cloves, homegrown roasted potatoes, French-style green beans, freshly baked dinner rolls, and for dessert, the nickname that Albert gave to her after their first date on May 4, 1971: apple dumplings.

The two had met in Baltimore, Maryland. Agnes was working as a lab technician at a biochemical company, and Albert had just finished a four-year stint in the Navy. The chemistry, Agnes would later joke because of her job position, was there from the start. She was 32, and Albert was 25.

Albert landed a job as a sales consultant for the same company, and so they saw each other often—except when he had to fly to California, or Texas, or the Midwest for a growers convention. His good looks and charming personality quickly escalated him to head of sales. The two bought a nice summer home near the Eastern Shore, and it wasn't unusual for them to spend their rare free time walking the many beaches and boardwalks. But when Ocean City expanded in the 1980s, and summer tourists crowded the few highways leading up to the waterfront, they sold the home and moved to Annapolis, Maryland. That's where Agnes honed her interest in gardening.

She soon became a supporting member of the Federated Garden Clubs of Maryland, and over the years she achieved Master Gardener status. In her spare time she also taught horticulture classes at a few of the surrounding universities. Albert took an interest in indoor houseplants and outdoor container gardening as well. It was a beautiful, symbiotic relationship that blossomed more and more each year. The thought of living without Albert was unimaginable to Agnes.

Weeks went by after the funeral, and although a few of the neighbors showed up at the service, none of them reached out to Agnes afterward to help her through her immense grief. They looked at her like a weed that surrounded a once-beautiful flower. Something that needed to be plucked away as soon as possible.

Her wonderful garden, which had been a high-point of the neighborhood—and probably increased home values—fell into disrepair. Flower heads, once vibrant with color, drooped to the ground and turned a crusty brown. Invasive weeds crept into the flower beds and suffocated the ornate ground covering, making

PEOPLE WHO NEED TO DIE

the beds indistinguishable from the rest of the yard. High winds brought down small branches and twigs, which rotted into the soil and attracted hordes of insects and nesting rodents. Dead coy rose to the surface of the back pond and wafted a fishy stench throughout the neighborhood. A few of the sculptures tumbled off their stone mounts and smashed into oddly shaped pieces. David's penis rested on the edge of the pond, while his head, which now stared ominously at the back of the house, rolled in the opposite direction.

Agnes herself stayed inside most of the time. If it weren't for someone occasionally spotting her out for her mail, they might have thought she had died as well. One neighbor shouted from across the street one morning that her yard was an eyesore to the community. Agnes sent a focused stare over to the woman, Heidi Cockstead, then turned and slowly made her way back inside. After that she waited until the cover of night to retrieve her letters.

Six long years went by. The neighbors waited, like cold-hearted hyenas on the watch, to rid themselves of that old woman for good. Realtors, professional house-flippers, and independent home-renovation businesses stuck pamphlets in her door. At one time the county considered fining Agnes for unkempt and potentially hazardous premises.

But then a young man mysteriously showed up in the late spring of 2021, and the neighbors couldn't take their eyes off him.

He wore tight black shorts that cupped his firm ass and continued to mid-thigh, where a white band bordered the taut material and his lightly tanned skin. His shirtless torso revealed a large chest, rolling abs, and arms thick as boas. His short hair was dark and wavy, and his face looked military: firm jaw, inset eyes, and a sly smile. He looked like one of those farm-boy wrestler types where hard work and half a gallon of milk a day did a body good.

The sound of the hammer hitting nails didn't bother the neighbors at all. It was their cue to part the curtains, pull up a chair, and watch God's finest creation at work. And it began every day at nine o'clock sharp, and ended roughly around four. The seven-foot-high wood fence started at the property line by the street and gradually made its way around Agnes' backyard. Every now and then the muscled hunk would rest against the truck tailgate, down a full bottle of water, and wipe the sweat off his pecs with a T-shirt he never wore. Then he'd lift another pallet-size fence section overhead and carry it to where he left off. His calves flexed and bulged as he walked, and Rich Logan from across the way dreamt about sniffing the black sneakers he wore on his bare feet.

The fence erection continued for several weeks, three weeks and two days to be exact, Emily Pearson counted. She and the others wondered who this young man was, and if they could conjure up work for him on their own properties. Anything to get closer to that wonderful body. But before they could summon the courage to approach the God of Dairy Goodness, the job had been completed and he disappeared.

Fencing now surrounded the entire perimeter of Agnes' property. All that was visible was a portion of the second floor of her house. Occasionally, a figure could be seen moving past an upstairs window. Perhaps Agnes had slipped away in the night, or some close relative moved her to a nursing home. And then new owners had moved in and would be renovating the place. Maybe, Emily hoped and occasionally orgasmed over, the new owner *was* the muscle boy! Whatever the circumstances, the neighbors were grateful not to have to look at that hideous yard anymore.

And then the unusual trucks arrived.

Cyan Botanicals was the name on the magnetic sign attached to the white van that arrived three days later. A curved green leaf accentuated the logo. A box truck with Mystery Aquatics painted on the side came soon after. Two men unloaded heavy, round containers. Next came Gracious Herbaceous, followed by Carnivore Creations. Then there were the mulch trucks, which made perfect sense, arriving at the back gate and unloading several cubic yards of the rich-smelling compost.

"I just *have* to know what's going on over there!" Rich blurted at one of Janet Mitchell's social gatherings.

"I'm sure the new owners are just cleaning up that mess Agnes made." Janet sipped her bloodred Merlot. She remembered working with Agnes at the Maryland Horticultural Center decades ago.

"Has anyone seen anyone coming in or out of the house?" Emily Pearson added. "I sure hope it's that hot—um, I wonder if that guy that put up the fence moved in."

"Do you think it's his place?" Patricia Livingston dipped a cracker into the garlic humus and devoured it in one bite. "What's the word, Heidi? You always seem to be up on the latest gossip."

"I've heard nothing. But whoever it is, they must like gardening, too. I do have a feeling our dear old Agnes has flown the coop."

"Yes, I think so as well." Janet poured herself another glass of wine, then offered the same to her guests. "A toast. To our new neighbor, whoever he or she may be."

"To our new neighbor."

"Yes, our neighbor."

"To anyone but Agnes."

The group laughed, clanked their glasses together, then looked out the picture window at the tall white fence—now cast in a bluish hue from the summer moonlight—that separated them from the answer within.

One: Betrayal

You are cordially invited to dinner tonight, July 5, 2021, at 6 p.m. Let's keep this our little secret. Your new neighbor, Matt.

Janet Mitchell discovered the small invitation card inside her door after returning home from grocery shopping a week later. At first she thought it was a clever ad for a local restaurant. Then she noticed the man across the street leaning against the fence. She nearly dropped both bags. Matt raised his arm and subtly wiggled his fingers at her. It was the hunk after all! This time he wore a form-fitting gray shirt and knee-length white shorts. His hair was slicked back to reveal thick black eyebrows, and his eyes seemed to reach across the distance for her. Janet smiled and raised the card to let him know she saw it. Matt nodded back, then opened the front gate and disappeared from view. It took two minutes and a leaky milk carton for Janet to realize she hadn't moved from the doorway.

A green blouse and black shorts was the final outfit she chose for the clandestine occasion. It was already five thirty and a few of the other neighbors had returned home. Patricia would be watching the six o'clock news. Heidi and Emily would be at yoga class until seven, and Rich was probably sipping his nighttime martini while puttering around his backyard. She made her escape at precisely 5:59 p.m.

"Hi, I'm glad you could come tonight." Matt opened up the front gate just as Janet approached. He had watched and waited for her.

"Hi, I'm Janet Mitchell." Janet smiled, then felt a tingle when Matt's muscled arm brushed against her back as he closed the gate behind them. "We've been wondering who moved in here. Is this your place now?"

"Yes." The two stood in the grassless front yard. "You'll have to excuse this area here. I haven't done much but clear away the brush and remove some large roots." Janet noticed four or five dug-up areas. Matt put his arm around her before she could speak again and guided her toward the side yard. "Come with me. We'll dine out back tonight."

Tall rose bushes with bright red blooms lined the walkway. Some of the petals had fallen to the ground, adding to the romantic mood of the evening. Janet couldn't believe that this young man would be interested in her, of all people. He was probably in his mid-twenties, less than half her age. She hadn't seen a man this handsome since that guy she had a fling with at the Prince William County Fair back in 2016. Brad was his name. But even he lacked the social grace and homegrown beauty of the man she was with tonight.

"Wow, what a wonderful setup." In the middle of the backyard sat a round table covered with an embroidered white cloth. Atop were two place settings: porcelain plates with gold trim, silver utensils, and large wine goblets. A clear glass vase in the center held two large red roses. A dozen six-foot-high stone obelisks surrounded the table area like a mini Stonehenge. Other parts of the backyard were blocked off with more fencing.

"Thank you." Matt guided Janet between two of the pillars and pulled out her chair for her. "Have a seat."

"I can't get over how much you've done in such a short time. These stones must have been hell to lift and put in place."

"Yeah, it was a bit of work. But I had a little help."

"What was your inspiration for this design?"

Matt sat in the chair across from her. "The National Monument, partly. But I also like how the sharp points and the circular design give it a medieval feel. Plus, you can tell time with it."

"Oh, so it's like a sundial, too?" A shadow from one of the obelisks crossed over Janet's left eye.

"Yes, and right now it's half past beautiful." Matt rose up to pour the wine. Janet blushed.

"I've been watching you watching me, Janet. And I knew from the start that you were someone I wanted to get to know better." Matt placed the glass in Janet's hand.

"Oh my. I don't know what to say. I mean, I'm a bit

embarrassed that you noticed me watc—"

"Don't be embarrassed. I'm glad you saw me. I'm glad you like what you see. But I want to know more about you." Matt sat back down and sipped from his glass as if he were drinking from Janet herself. His eyes never left her.

"Well, I'm just a woman, who likes gardens, and good food, and...."

"You married?"

"I was. But that was years ago. No...I've just been...waiting, I guess."

"Waiting is always the hardest part, isn't it? Waiting for the right person, waiting to get ahead in life. It seems life is nothing more than waiting for the next best thing to happen."

"You are *so* right. How is it that you're this wise at such a young age? May I ask how old you are?"

"Age doesn't really matter, does it Janet? I'm old enough to know what I like. And I like you."

Janet felt another tingle inside. She pulled the wine goblet up to her mouth to conceal her sheepish grin. Matt relieved her from the moment.

"Now, I've made chicken breasts covered with homegrown mushrooms and smothered in a garlic wine sauce. It's good for you, and good tasting. I should have asked. You do like mushrooms, don't you?"

"Yes, I love them. I don't have them as often as I'd like. I tried to grow my own, too, but never had much success."

"It's easy. I'll show you mine after we eat. I grow a special kind." Matt scooped a breast onto Janet's plate, then added a side of grilled vegetables glazed with balsamic vinegar."

"This looks wonderful. Not many guys I know like to cook, except Rich. But he's gay, so, you know."

"I feel it's important to know what you put in your body. Fresh food keeps you fresh and in good spirits."

Janet watched Matt's large bicep flex as he set down the

vegetable dish and returned to his chair. She couldn't get the image out of her head of him embracing her with those sinewy arms.

"Let's eat." Matt started with the vegetables, while Janet cut into the chicken."

"Oh." Janet paused and slowly chewed. "This is delicious."

"Can you taste the garlic? I hope I didn't put too much in."

"No, no, it's fine. The mushrooms, though. They have such a lively punch to them. And the texture. They don't feel like typical mushrooms, slimy and such. They just make the meal come alive." Janet chewed a little more, then cut off another piece. "Yes, yes, I'll have to get this recipe from you."

Fifteen minutes went by without much talking. While the sun set and a string of lights cut on above them, Janet engulfed the chicken as if she hadn't eaten in a week. Matt leaned back and picked through his vegetables. Occasionally, he'd hold his wine glass to his mouth and send seductive and inquisitive glances her way. Finally, he broke the silence.

"So tell me about the woman who lived here before me."

"Oh, Agnes." Janet swallowed the last piece of chicken and wiped her mouth with her napkin. "Well, she was an old woman, who had a nice garden at one time. But then she let it go to pot."

"Did you know her well?" Matt sipped some of his wine.

"Well, as much as I wanted to know her. We worked together, many years ago, at a horticultural center in Maryland. She started before I did. Anyway, I came in and they picked me to be the Assistant Director of Research. It was a position Agnes was hoping to get."

"Do you know why they didn't pick her?"

"She certainly deserved it. The lady was brilliant. And she knew what she was talking about. She had a degree in Botany. But," Janet smiled a coy smile, "the head of the department and I had sort of an understanding."

"What was that?"

"Well, I was young back then, and quite flirty. I didn't have the experience Agnes had, but I knew how to get ahead, so to speak." Janet raised her glass and sipped the wine. "Oof, this wine is making me a bit dizzy."

"Sip it slower." Matt stood up from his chair and walked over behind Janet. She felt his fingers begin to knead at her shoulders. "That's all in the past."

"Yes, but I don't think Agnes ever got over it. She was like a thorn in my side. But, it is what it is, you know. I didn't want to play the waiting game, to get a promotion. So I did what I felt I had to."

"That's right. And look at you now. A beautiful woman, sitting with me, here, in my garden."

Janet's head spun like a merry-go-round. She grabbed her napkin to wipe the beads of sweat off her forehead. Matt continued to massage her shoulders. His firm hands ventured up along the sides of her neck a few times.

"Oh, wow. I'm feeling...." Janet stood up. "I'm feeling so, wow, like..." The obelisks seemed to dance in front of her eyes like characters in an old cartoon. Then items on the table chimed in. The knives and forks grew faces and smiled back at her.

"Maybe you just need to walk it off." Matt turned her toward him, kissed her on the lips, then stepped back a few feet. "Come toward me, Janet."

Janet took one step, and it was as if she had no feet. Then another. The wind blew over her face, contorting it into the weird, cockeyed look you'd see on a mental patient.

"I feel so...so spacey, and happy, and..."

"It's the mushrooms, Janet. My own special blend for our special time together. Now, come toward me." Matt hopped a few obelisks over.

Janet turned left and aimed to where Matt had landed. She took two quick steps forward, almost losing her balance.

"Run to me, Janet. See if you can catch me." Matt walked

around the outside edge of the stone pillars, stopping briefly between each one. Janet circled the perimeter of the table and giggled.

"I'm over her, Janet."

Janet began to pick up speed.

"I want you, Janet. I want you in my arms. To hold you tightly, night after night. You just need to get to me."

"Stop it." Janet laughed. "You're being such a wonderful tease, and I love it."

"Run to me now. Chase your dreams, Janet. Climb to the top!"

Janet lunged toward Matt a split second after he moved behind another obelisk. Then he reappeared. His body stretched and warped in her vision like a reflection in a carnival mirror. "You're almost to me. One more time, Janet. Run to me!"

Janet sprinted straight toward Matt, who now stood only six steps away. But the dancing obelisks confused her again. He opened his big arms wide, and she spread hers too, with eyes closed, as if the moment she had dreamt about earlier was about to happen. And it would have, had her face not collided with the hard surface of one of the pillars like Wile E. Coyote hitting the side of a cliff. As she slid down the stone front, leaving a bloody trail in the process, Matt moved over to where she came to rest.

"Almost, Janet. You almost had me."

She saw the roses again that night, at least the silhouettes of them, against the stormy gray sky. She felt the bare skin of her back scrape along the cold stone path, and her blouse glide up to her neck with every forceful tug. In a matter of minutes the stars disappeared, the din of nighttime bugs muffled away, and a blanket of something heavy and wet silenced her attempts to scream.

Two: Gossip

Care to join me for a swim? July 6, 2021, at 4 p.m. Bathing suit optional. Your new neighbor, Matt.

Heidi pulled the invitation card from her car window and almost tossed it away before her eyes caught a glimpse of the man across the street wearing nothing more than a tight blue Speedo. Matt was leaning against his fence with his muscled arms folded together and his right calf crossed over his left thigh in a figure-four configuration. He tipped his head up toward her and smiled, grabbed a towel and swung it over his shoulder, then slipped through the fence gate. She almost wet herself right there.

This time the backyard was sectioned off so only a large circular pool with a four-foot cascading waterfall was visible. Decorative stone urns overflowing with red geraniums and trailing ivies surrounded part of the perimeter. A small table with a silver ice bucket holding a bottle of vintage Chardonnay sat off to the side. Heidi cautiously entered the gate and followed the directional "Pool Party for Two" signs Matt had placed along the pathway.

"Hello." Heidi paused a few feet from the side of the pool when she noticed Matt's muscular back glistening in the water. He turned around and smiled. Tiny droplets of water at the ends of his dark eyelashes flickered in the afternoon sunlight.

"Hi there." Matt ran his hand over his dripping wet hair and pulled himself over to the pool edge. Then he raised himself out with his arms. Heidi turned away for a moment and covered her eyes, thinking he might be au naturel. Matt smiled again and ran his hands along the sides of his swim trunks. "I'm glad you could make it."

"This was a nice surprise for me, getting your invitation. I've been wanting to know who moved in here. And it's you, after all. I'm Heidi."

"Matt. It's nice to meet you, Heidi." Matt moved over to the side table. "Would you like some wine?"

"Yes, thank you. That would be nice." Heidi set down her towel and took the glass in her hand. Matt leaned into her and poured the frothy liquid. She wanted to rest her head on his bare chest right then and there. The two sat down at the edge of the pool and dipped their feet in the water.

"This is amazing," Heidi continued. "This used to be a coy pond, but I see you've enlarged it enough to make it a nice wading pool. And still it doesn't take up a whole lot of space. What's that over there?" Heidi pointed to a corner of the backyard surrounded by more fencing.

"Just another area I'm working on. I like to partition off what's still in progress." Matt looked directly into Heidi's eyes, then down to her breasts. "Nice swimsuit."

"Thanks." Heidi smiled and leaned back onto her forearms. Her long red hair fell backward. "So you like what you see?"

"I *do* like what I see. You're certainly not a work-in-progress. I'd say you're completely done. Perfection."

Heidi pulled the wine glass up to her lips, then rested it on her bare midriff.

"I'm so glad you moved in. The woman who lived here before. You don't even want to know."

Matt turned to his side and propped his head up with his big arm. "Tell me about her."

"Well," Heidi laughed, "I always thought she was a lesbian. She hung out with women more than men. At least the gardening kind. Sure, I have a garden, too, but I do get out and involve myself with the opposite sex."

"Was she married?"

"Agnes? Yes, she was married to a very attractive man, Albert. He died several years back. Then we only saw Agnes a few times. Do you know what happened to her?"

"I don't." Matt sipped from his glass and smiled.

140

"I used to tell people Agnes was probably frigid. With a man like that, I don't think I'd leave the bedroom."

"Ooo, you *are* a little troublemaker." Matt sat up and set his glass to the side. "How about we cause a *stir* in the water...and maybe some other places?" He jumped into the pool and swiped a splash of water up toward her with his right arm.

"You!" Heidi laughed and sat upright. Matt bobbed around a few times.

"The water is nice. Come on in!"

"Let me drink a bit more wine. I like watching you."

Matt flexed his upper body as if he were a contestant in the first underwater bodybuilding competition. Then he swam over to Heidi and tickled her feet. She laughed and tried to pull her legs up.

"C'mon now. I've got something to show you." Matt backstroked to the center of the pool, then paused. He smiled back at Heidi, ran his hands over his hair, then reached into the water. A few seconds later he raised his left hand with the pair of blue Speedos in his grip. He twirled them around his finger a few times before tossing them to the pool edge.

Heidi stood up and unclasped her bikini top. She slowly entered the pool and waited until the water was just above her chest before pulling it off.

"Nice." Matt bobbed in the center.

Heidi reached below the water surface, laughed at Matt's gaga expression, then tossed her bikini bottom poolside.

"Bottoms up!" She slowly approached Matt, dunking her head underwater to wet her hair, before resurfacing inches away from his face. Matt brought his arms around her waist and kissed her softly on the lips.

"Wait!" Matt swam to the edge of the pool and pulled himself out. "We need some party music." Heidi seemed shocked by the sudden exit, but the sight of Matt's incredible nude physique tamed her reaction.

"Nice ass!" she playfully shouted.

A few minutes later a pounding, repetitive beat picked up through the surrounding speakers. It was almost a little too loud, Heidi thought, but she knew their bodies would do most of the talking.

Matt returned and refilled his glass of wine. His large cock dangled hypnotically in front of her. As he sipped the wine and smiled back at her, a shimmering red cascade of small, indistinguishable creatures slid down the waterfall. Heidi was unaware of what was entering the pool behind her.

"Are you coming back in?" she said wistfully.

"I just want to watch you for a moment." Matt moved closer to the pool and winked.

Heidi began to mimic Matt's earlier flexing—until the first one bit her in the leg.

"Ouch! What the hell was that?"

The next bites didn't come until thirty seconds later. From then on it was non-stop. It felt as though a thousand staples had shot into her flesh. Then bits and pieces of her severed skin rose to the surface along thin trails of blood. Heidi screamed as the aggressive red-bellied piranhas attacked her legs, arms, and torso.

"What the hell have you done to me! You bastard! You sicko!"

"Those are some pretty biting comments, Heidi." Matt folded his arms and watched as Heidi flailed about. The agitated water around her body looked as if it were boiling during the frenzy. Matt lowered his hand momentarily to his engorged member. Her demise had a certain erotic pleasure to it.

Two minutes later Heidi's feeble wails ceased. The only sound after was the melodic music that served as backdrop to the feeding. Her half-chewed corpse bobbed up and down in the center like a large tuna after a shark onslaught. Matt guided the mass over to the side with a long pool net. He wrapped what was left of Heidi into a large tarpaulin, then dragged her away.

As the sun set, Matt finished the bottle of wine and laid naked on his back in front of the pool. He tossed leftover bits of chicken to the ferocious feasters and replayed the evening in his head several times before finishing himself off.

Three: Adultery

It was her nature to stray. Patricia Livingston had had affairs with just about everyone's husband in Lake Jackson. She attributed her attractiveness to her soft, smooth skin. Even in her fifties it still retained a certain porcelain luminescence. She had a glow about her, men would say, and it made her infallibly irresistible to them. Including Albert.

On the day Pat helped Albert weed out a patch of Virginia creeper, Agnes was off teaching a class on, ironically, keeping native pervasives in check. The two had started up a conversation about high school sweethearts, and Patricia talked emphatically about her first kiss. Joey Johnston, the high school prom king, had taken her into the shed behind her home in rural Connecticut. After a bit of coy resistance on her part, he held her wrists together between them and slowly laid one on her. It was an incredible feeling, that thrill of lips meeting lips for the first time, and one that she sought to repeat often.

After she and Albert had finished in the garden, he brought out a pitcher of his spirituous homemade lemonade. The two walked around the back, making note of Agnes' work without mentioning her name, when they found themselves under the secluded latticework of an arbor. The sweet smell of the honeysuckle that strung overhead and cascaded around them seemed to beckon the moment. He gracefully placed his right hand under her chin, leaned in with eyes closed, and held fast to her lips for nearly twenty seconds.

But it didn't go much further than that.

Albert loved Agnes dearly, and it would be the only time he'd slip up. Agnes forgave him, which somehow brought the two closer. She never confronted Patricia about it. By then Pat had already fervently pursued locking lips with Emily Pearson's ex-husband, Roy.

Matt caught Patricia unloading a tray of flowers from the back of her Subaru wagon the day after Heidi Cockstead tumbled down the food chain.

"I see you seem to be a rather skilled gardener," Matt said before entering his front gate. Patricia immediately honed in on the kissable dimple above Matt's upper lip.

"Hi. Oh, I do my best. Is this your new place?" Pat walked over to Matt with a few pots in her hands. He was even better looking close up.

"It is. I'm working on cleaning up the front and back. Maybe you can help me decide what to plant out back. I'm awful when it comes to landscaping. But I know how to build fences."

"Yes, we saw—or rather, I can see that. It's great that you want to turn the place back into something nice to look at. Do you have a time frame in mind?"

"Well, I could use some help this afternoon, if you're not too busy."

"Sure, let me go put these inside, and I'll come on over."

"Great. Oh, my name is Matt."

"Hi Matt. Patricia. Patricia Livingston."

Patricia skirted back to her car and removed the last two trays of perennials. A summer sale at Home Depot's garden center had her overspending once again. A couple of select plants would make a nice neighborly welcome, she thought.

Around one o'clock in the afternoon, when the sun was at its peak, Patricia knocked on Matt's gate.

"I brought you something," she said, the light reflecting off her pale skin with almost a halo effect.

"Oh wow, thanks. Let me carry those for you." Matt reached

out his arms to take the two full trays. For a moment his warm hands brushed over hers. She envisioned him dropping the trays right there and planting one on her. But, as with the others, she knew it was the journey to the kiss that made it most alluring. Immediacy would mean mediocrity.

The backyard now had both the obelisk and pool areas hidden from view. In between was a ten-foot pathway.

"This is where I'd like to plant. It gets full sun, as you can see, so do you think those will do okay?"

"Oh yes, these will be perfect. Do you have a trowel?"

"Yes. Let me go get a couple." Matt entered the back door of the house.

While he was gone, Pat poked around a bit. The arbor where she had shared a kiss with Albert had long been removed. The weight of the honeysuckle and the wet, humid summers surely took it down. In its place a hazy plastic sheet surrounded what looked like some sort of tall shrub or bush. It was hard to tell with the bright reflections of the afternoon sunlight. At one point she thought she saw it move.

"Here we go." Matt returned just as she was about to peek around the plastic.

"What's this?"

"It's nothing, just a sapling I planted." Matt softly grabbed Pat's hand and guided her back to the planting area. "Your skin is so light; you must wear some sun protection."

"Oh, I have on 50 SPF full-spectrum sunscreen. I do everything to keep my skin soft and supple."

"I can see, and it looks very nice." Matt smiled and handed Pat one of the two trowels. He purposely ran his fingers over hers. "But I insist you try this, too." He pulled from his short's pocket a small unlabeled bottle filled with a milky, creamy substance. "It's a formula my aunt used to make. And she had radiant skin all her life, just like yours."

"Really? What's it made of?"

"Just botanical extracts. They work with the protein in your skin cells."

Pat leaned over and smelled the open bottle.

"Oh, that's nice. Okay, I'll try it."

She rested the trowel on the edge of the pathway, then poured a little of the lotion onto her palms. Matt watched as she ran her hands up and down her arms, front and back. Then she generously applied the lotion to her bare legs.

"Use as much as you want. Don't forget your face. This afternoon sun can be harsh."

Pat poured out a bit more, rubbed her hands together, and smoothed the cream over her forehead, cheeks, nose and neck.

"There, now you're protected. Go ahead and keep the bottle. It's my gift to you."

"Thank you. I love the way it feels on me."

"It will feel better once it's fully absorbed."

The two began the plantings. Matt kept his distance by working on the opposite end. She'd gaze over to him and imagine how his strong lips would feel against hers. Twenty minutes later a row of bright purple asters was flanked on both sides by short, wispy grasses.

"There. Now that's a good start." Pat leaned back and tried to figure out a segue into her plan. Perhaps she would invite him over to her place. Edward was on a business trip and wouldn't be back until Monday. Seducing a man in the confines of her own property had a delightful taboo to it.

"How would you like to come look at my rear garden this evening?" She handed the trowel back to Matt and stacked the two empty trays together. "I'm going to plant what I bought today over the next hour or so, and then clean up."

"That would be nice." Matt sensed her ulterior motive. "Is your husband away?"

"Yes, he went to South Carolina on business. He'll be gone several more days."

146

"Then I would love to, Patricia." Matt paused. "If you could, let's keep this to ourselves. We don't want the neighbors talking."

"I fully agree." Pat smiled as Matt walked her to the front yard and opened the gate. She reached out her hand to shake his, but Matt just flirtatiously leaned his face against the gate and spoke in a soft but masculine tone.

"I'll see you soon."

One hour later was precisely when it took effect. Normally contact with the toxic sap of the Giant Hogweed plant rendered severe burns and eventual blindness within minutes. But the time-release concoction Matt provided to Pat bided her a few more moments with her lovely, adulteress skin.

She thought it was bug bites. Then blisters the size of quarters formed along her forearms and on the tops of her hands. Next, her thighs felt as if they were on fire, and not in the good way. Soon they, too, were covered with pus-oozing sores. The pain was so excruciating that when she tried to stand up, she instantly collapsed onto the bed of flowers she had just planted.

Under the watchful eyes from her neighbor's second floor, Pat writhed uncontrollably for several minutes. She was able to utter two small shrills, squeaks actually, before large blisters broke open on her face and fused her lips together. Then came her eyesight. Had she not rubbed her hands over her eyes to remove the sweat minutes before, it may have been spared. Now she found herself crawling aimlessly in her secluded back garden to get out of the sun, her once-alabaster skin patinaed into a crusty red rust. It was a hideous ending.

When her movements dwindled to mere twitches, Matt crept over to Patricia's back yard, carefully rolled her in tarpaulin with gloved hands, and inconspicuously carried her through a small opening in his back fence.

Four: Stealing

It was experimental. It had never been done before. It was otherworldly eerie, like something out of a B movie. But there it was, all twelve feet of it, in Matt's backyard. And it was hungry.

Diamonds are a best friend's girls. That was the twist Emily Pearson put on the famous Marilyn Monroe line after sneaking out a pair of Agnes' treasured diamond earrings while attending a dinner party at her home. Agnes was her best friend at the time, and somehow she felt those "girls" suited her better. Had she asked, Agnes would have gladly loaned them to her.

Her obsession with everything that sparkled began at age four. Her father had returned from a week overseas, and one of his gifts to her was a small apple-shaped broach decked out with shimmering stones. They were fake diamonds, of course; she was just a kid. But she quickly believed that she deserved nothing less. If it didn't reflect light at a million angles, it wasn't worth her time. Walking into her bedroom as an adult you'd think she hoarded the Walmart jewelry department. All the living room furniture was either brass or chrome, and the walls were covered with mirrors. And she was the only person Agnes knew who had a chandelier in every room.

"My god, lady, is it really necessary to have a chandelier in the crapper?" Roy would say every time he hit his head and jostled the glass crystals. When Emily insisted he wear a pair of shimmering gold lamé underwear during lovemaking, Roy drew the line. "Lady, if just being around me isn't enough to put a shine in you, then I'm outta here."

And so he went.

A rhinestone-studded mirror with bovine horns on top was the bait Matt used to lure Emily onto his property. He was removing the large monstrosity from his truck when she walked by on her way home.

"Wow, that's a magnificent mirror. Where did you get it?"

"Just an old hand-me-down from my father. He was a bull rider in Texas and he won this as a prize. It sat out in our garage for years. Figured I'd give it a place in the living room."

"Oh, so this *is* your place." Emily crossed the street and held out her hand. She subtly checked herself in the mirror. Yep, everything was in place.

"Hi, I'm Matt." Matt set down the mirror and reached back. Like the others, Emily quivered inside when his fingers wrapped around hers.

"Hey, you wouldn't happen to have seen my friends, Patricia and Heidi? Pat lives next door, and Heidi has long red hair."

"Yes. I think I may have a few days ago. But I've been working inside so much I haven't been able to be very social. You're the first person I've spoken to."

"Oh jeez, and I haven't even told you my name. I'm Emily. Emily Pearson."

"Pleased to meet you, Emily." Matt smiled and saw that Emily was eyeing his crotch while they shook. The lure and capture always caused a nice stir down there. "Would you like to come inside? I could use a good eye to hang this straight."

"Yeah. Sure. I guess I could do that. I got a few minutes." She had all the time in the world, for him.

"Okay, thanks." Matt raised the hefty mirror onto his shoulders, and that's when Emily saw his muscled biceps up close. A large wet stain also drenched the back of his T-shirt like an image from a Rorschach test. She wanted to see that sweat glisten on his raw, shirtless body. He carried the mirror inside while she followed close behind.

"Okay. This is where I'd like to put it." Matt set the mirror down and pointed to the empty spot above the fireplace. "Would you like a glass of wine before we get started?"

"This early in the day? Absolutely." Emily had taken up

drinking as a new hobby.

While Matt was away in the kitchen, she noticed a few of Agnes' old furniture pieces strewn around the living room. The floral-patterned settee she once sat in, the round mahogany table off to the side, and the antique grandfather clock with the brass pendulum Agnes and Albert had received as a wedding gift—all were still there.

"Here." Matt handed Emily her wine glass. A glint of light reflected off the liquid.

"Some of this furniture belonged to Agnes. In fact, a lot of it."

"I acquired the house as is." Matt moved closer to her, standing right in her face while sipping from his glass."

"So what happened to Agnes?"

"The woman that lived here before me?"

"Yes. That old batalac."

"I heard she died." Matt placed his hand on Emily's shoulder. "I hope seeing her stuff doesn't upset you?"

Emily felt the pressure of his grip on her. He kneaded her neck a few times before pulling away. It worked.

"No. I'm fine." She downed half the glass in one long gulp.

"So let's put this thing up here." Matt pulled a small stepping stool over to the fireplace and raised the gaudy mirror. "How's this?"

"Little higher, and a little to the left."

"Now?" His bulging crotch was at face height.

"Perfect."

He marked the spot with a black pen, tapped in a couple of heavy-duty hooks, then hung the mirror in place.

"There. Adds a more masculine touch to the room, you think?"

"Definitely." Emily was already feeling the effects of the wine. In fact, it had a firm hold on her. Matt noticed her pupils dilating. She was almost ready for his surprise.

"How about we go out back. I want to show you something."

Matt put his arm around Emily and guided her past a workhorse in the kitchen and out the back door.

It was a clear, bright day outside. Reflections off the white fencing were almost blinding. Emily raised her forearm to shadow her face. A slight breeze transported a sweet, intoxicating aroma with a subtle hint of decay.

"Wow, you've got something going on out here. What's with all the fences?"

"Work in progress. Come. It's in the far back."

After Patricia's pitiful perishing, Matt had finished laying down an intricate cobblestone pathway that curved around various empty plant beds. The spaces between the decorative rocks were inlaid with blue and gold ceramic fragments, which swirled together in a mesmerizing scheme. It made a tipsy Emily more unsteady.

"Wow, this is like, *amazing*. It's like a version of the yellow brick road. Only blue, and gold, and shiny, and...and beautiful."

"And it all leads to the land of Oz. Come now, let me hold your hand." Matt slowly pulled Emily along.

"Please tell me there are ruby slippers at the end."

"Almost. I think you'll be quite happy."

Along the way Emily observed her distorted reflections in the dozens of opulent gazing globes lining the path. She felt like Alice in Wonderland on crack. She teetered and tottered and almost lost her balance a few times. Twenty steps later Matt released her hand. The view in front of her left her awestruck.

"It's called the Giant Jewel Plant or Drosera Monstera."

Thousands of glistening red orbs the size of golf balls adorned the ends of foot-long tentacles, which covered the surface of nearly a dozen elongated leaves. Mucilage secretions dripped off the deep-red tips like a sugary nectar. Some of the leaves were rolled up at the ends; most were unfurled. The entire plant towered above Emily nearly two-people high.

"Oh my lord." It was as if she had found the Holy Grail of

Shimmer. "I've never seen such a beautiful thing!"

"Go ahead. Get closer."

Emily stepped to within a foot away.

"Can you smell it?" Matt prodded. "It's very tasty. Run your fingers through the clear sap."

Emily reached out her hand. She looked back at Matt and smiled like Eve about to take the apple.

"Go ahead."

At first the bulbous fruit felt squishy and wet. But when she tried to pull her hand free, an elastic strand of the sticky substance pulled it back in. Her hand attached itself like crazy glue.

"What IS this!"

Next, an entire leaf, two in fact, swooped down from the sky and wrapped around her shoulders and her legs. More sticky tentacles attached themselves to her skin. As the giant plant lifted Emily off the ground, she noticed the carcass of a crow rolled into the center of another leaf.

"It's a carnivorous plant, you stupid bitch. Don't you know your species? It's the sundew, grown exceptionally big, for you."

Her toiling brought on more tentacles, which wrapped around her feet, arms, and neck. Goo strands attached to her hair, splaying it apart like a wig set out to dry. Sticky balls pressed against her cheeks and pulled the skin of her face in opposite directions. Within minutes her entire body was coated with the steadfast glue.

"Quite a sticky situation, huh, Emily?"

She couldn't speak. A glistening tentacle had sealed her mouth shut.

Matt left and returned with his glass of wine. He rested on the stone path and watched the spectacle play out in front of him. If only Emily could see how beautiful she looked up there thrashing about. It was as if she were encased in diamonds.

Fifteen minutes later her movements were no more. The

viscous globules began secreting enzymes to facilitate digestion. Matt put his hand up to his ear and listened closely, the breeze having died down.

He could almost hear the slurping.

Five: Murder

He barely felt the bump, but the squeal would remain in his head all day.

Rich Logan had been adjusting the dial of his classic 1967 Dodge Coronet radio while driving down Macintosh Lane on July 9, 2011. Tuning an old AM/FM receiver in the digital era was akin to dial-up Internet. It took time and patience. Somewhere between 89.1 and 92.3, the car jarred slightly upward. A muffled screech, a tiny howling of sort, resounded. He thought it was high-frequency radio interference. Then he looked in his rearview mirror.

He had run over Agnes Woodward's two-year-old Scottish terrier.

He slowed down for a moment, unsure of how to handle the situation. Bonnie tried to pull herself up, even though both hind legs were shattered. Her little head rocked from side to side with each failed attempt. She panted for several minutes while Rich idled in his car.

What would Agnes say if she found out he hit her dog? How would she treat him? Would he still be invited to her yearly Christmas parties known for their fine cuisine and extravagant parting gifts? Last year she gave out expensive bottles of wine and personalized cutting boards.

Bonnie's panting soon turned to wheezing. Lying on her side caused undue pressure on her lungs. The hot overhead sun beat down where she rested. Had Rich turned around and sought help, the poor thing might have stood a chance. Instead, he tuned to an '80s pop station and quickly drove away.

Bananarama's "Cruel Summer" played through the speakers while little Bonnie slowly exited the world.

A lawn chair, the same pair of tight black trunks he wore on the first day, and bare feet crossed at the ankles was all it took for Matt to lure Rich as he drove by his house. The front gate was wide open. Rich popped the curb and nearly crashed into the fence.

Matt jumped up like a trapdoor spider.

"Are you okay?" He stopped at the edge of the gate. Rich tried to put the car in reverse, but the lever was stuck. Matt walked over and leaned his bare torso into the passenger side. Rich breathed in his strong, musky odor. It was hypnotic.

"It seems to be stuck. The lever won't move."

"I think you need to straighten out your wheel." Matt reached his thick arm across and pulled clockwise. His hand momentarily brushed against Rich's leg. "Try it again."

Rich shifted into Neutral, but "R" was still unachievable.

"Still stuck."

"Let me try."

Matt circled around to the driver's side. Rich stepped out. His face nearly brushed against Matt's chest. He eyed Matt's legs as he entered the car. They were spectacular. Matt jostled the wheel back and forth a few times, put his bare foot on the brake, then shifted the lever into reverse.

"There. Let me park the car. I want you to come inside."

Rich backed away while Matt maneuvered the car off the sidewalk and parked it along the curb. His heart was racing.

"Okay. There." Matt stepped from the car and reached out his hand. "Hi, I'm Matt."

Rich reveled in the long, firm grasp. "Rich Logan. Nice to finally meet you. I'm still a little shaken up. I didn't mean to drive up on your lawn."

"Don't worry about it. I'm sure the grass will grow back.

Would you like to come inside? "

"Sure, I'd like that. Very much." How could he say no?

Matt placed his hand on Rich's shoulder and led him through the gate. Once inside, he offered Rich a glass of wine, the same mixture that made the others so easily comply.

"Something to calm you down." Matt handed Rich the glass, then took a sip from his own.

"So you bought the house from Agnes?" Rich asked.

"Not exactly." Matt answered. "I acquired it."

"Oh, so did she pass away. Are you a relative?" Just then Rich noticed a picture of Agnes and Bonnie on a corner side table.

"Is she still here?" Rich swung around. Matt was standing right on him. Rich's eyes dropped to Matt's muscled pecs. Matt wrapped his free hand around the back of Rich's neck and pulled his face into them.

"Take a deep breath." Matt held him there for several seconds. Rich inhaled the potent, manly scent he noticed in the car. It was calming and intoxicating, like testosterone chloroform. "Now, let's go out back and get comfortable."

Like a lost puppy, Rich followed Matt through the house. He couldn't believe he was with this hot young man and what had just happened. Matt didn't seem to be gay. But why else would he do what he did?

It was an exceptionally warm day. The sun beat down on the twelve stone obelisks, which were now back in view. In the middle was a round blue mat with a white circle in the center. It looked like a mini-coliseum set up for an epic wrestling match.

"This is where I like to relax and stretch out." Matt sat in the center of the mat and set his wine glass off to the side.

"Oh, like yoga?"

"Yeah, sorta. Come sit in front of me."

Rich drank a long gulp of wine. The effects were almost immediate. He set his half-empty glass next to one of the obelisks, took off his shoes, then walked onto the mat.

"Here, right in front of me."

Rich began to sit Indian-style a few feet from Matt.

"No, the other way. Facing away from me," Matt commanded.

Rich swiveled around. His head took a moment to catch up.

"Like this?"

"Yeah. That's right."

Rich looked around at the semi-finished yard. "You've done a lot of work back here. What's over there behind the plas—"

Strong hands interrupted his words and began kneading the base of his neck.

"Don't speak. Don't say another thing." Matt's legs crept up on both sides of him.

"Oh, that feels so—"

"What did I just say?" Matt grasped a little harder. "You need to relax."

Matt continued the massage for several minutes. Rich's head wobbled back and forth from the pressure. He kept his eyes closed, until he felt the cool edge of a glass pressed up to his lips.

"Drink the rest of mine." Matt tilted the glass back while Rich rested his head on Matt's shoulder and sipped away. Matt placed his mouth up to Rich's ear and whispered. "That's right, take it all in."

Matt rolled the empty glass away, then continued the massage. Rich looked down and noticed Matt's fully extended legs on both sides of him. He relished the sight of those bulging calves, which now fluctuated in and out of focus.

"I want you to touch my legs, Rich."

Rich stretched his hands out and rested them just above Matt's knees.

"I want you to tell me what you feel."

Rich slowly caressed the massive thighs while Matt flexed them a couple of times.

"They're muscled, and smooth, with a little hair, and..."

Matt brought them closer against Rich. "And...?"

"And powerful. They feel powerful."

"Very good." Matt stopped kneading his neck for a moment. Rich felt his shirt bottom lift up. "Let's take this off you."

Rich extended his arms to the sky. Matt peeled the shirt free, then tossed it away. His hands resumed their work on Rich's shoulders.

"That feel better?" Matt continued.

"Yes....it feels...very, very good."

Matt's leaned in so his bare chest pressed against Rich's bare back. "Of course it does."

"I like your feet," suddenly escaped from Rich's mouth.

"These things?" Matt bent his left leg around Rich's chest so his foot rested on Rich's right hip. "Go ahead and touch it. Smell it if you want."

Rich curled his body forward and brought Matt's foot near his face. Matt pushed the back of Rick's head down into his sweaty sole and held him there for at least ten seconds. Rich almost suffocated in it.

"What's it smell like?" Matt loosened the grip on Rich's neck. Rich took a deep breath.

"Like grass...and soil...and like a man." Rich felt incredibly aroused.

"You like that, yeah?" Matt extended his leg back out and wiggled his toes. "Of course you do."

Before Rich could answer, Matt brought both legs around Rich's chest and crossed his ankles.

"Look what I else I can do with them, Rich. I can wrap them around you, and squeeze them, so you can feel that power you described. How's that?"

Rich buckled up a bit.

"It feels very nice."

"Would you like me to squeeze harder, Rich?"

"Yes...please do that." Rich was fixated on the flexing feet. Matt gripped tighter. His hamstrings were like ropes. Rich gasped a bit more air.

"Now Rich....what if I were to squeeze really, really tight?"

Rich reveled in the feeling of the young man's muscles around his nude torso. It was as if they could devour him. And who could say no to that?

"Go for it." Rich braced himself.

Matt snapped his inner thighs together and rolled Rich onto his side.

"How's that, Rich? Can you feel the pressure?"

Rich tried to speak, but lacked the air to form words.

"Hard to breathe, yes?" Matt flexed his glutes and straightened out. Rich grabbed Matt's thighs and tried to pry them off.

"Oh no. That's not gonna work, Rich. There's no turning back now." Matt cinched his legs tighter. Rich's ribcage cracked and a gust of air shot out of him.

"No turning back, which is exactly what you should have done when you ran over Agnes' dog ten years ago today. But you didn't, did you, Rich?"

Matt continued to bear down. Rich helplessly flailed his arms and legs about.

"No, Rich. You didn't. You didn't do the right thing." Matt loosened his grip, then clamped down at full strength. Rich had no time to inhale. Matt rolled him to his other side.

"How does it feel to be *crushed* to death?" Matt applied full pressure, like an anaconda in the heart of the Amazon constricting an unsuspecting capybara. Rich's eyes bulged from their sockets. His face turned beet red. Veins popped from his forehead. Strands of drool dripped from his mouth and glistened in the bright, scorching sun.

Killing Rich in this way aroused Matt more than all the others. Using his incredible body as the weapon made it all the more pleasurable. He watched his final victim slowly succumb to the iron embrace of his scissor hold. In a matter of minutes, Rich was out. His last glimpse in life was the cause of his demise. It was a beautiful sight. Dying at the legs of a hot hunk, whether a godsend or ironic payback for his cruel actions years ago, seemed like justifiable punishment. He let his body give in to it.

****

It was a full week before the cops arrived to investigate a missing-persons call. By then the white fence surrounding 224 Macintosh Lane had completely disappeared. Rich's car sat back in his driveway. And not a trace of evidence could be found. They even dredged the lake. It was as if half the neighborhood had disappeared. The only person remaining was dear Agnes Woodward. And who would suspect a sweet old lady?

The beds were beautiful that year, but even more so the next. In the spring and summer of 2022, the five mounds in Agnes' front yard flourished with robust perennials: bright red cannas, vibrant orange hibiscus, dazzling yellow rudbeckia, radiant pink peonies, and brilliant blue hydrangea. All were offset with lush, verdant grasses. In fact, it was the only garden on the block in bloom. Rotting flesh made the perfect fertilizer.

It was the rotten that got her application approved with the World Order Alliance. They permitted her small request to do what everyone dreams about now and then: rooting out the soulless and uncaring people—the liars, the cheaters, the gossipers, the stealers, the envious, and the frauds— who've done you wrong.

The serum she had formulated to keep her late husband Albert young and vibrant now flowed through the veins of another man. A very handsome and virile man. One who could woo anyone, man or woman, to his beckoning. One who would stake his claim on two hundred acres of land in rural Texas and raise a family of his own. One who would visit Agnes once a year to receive another injection.

"Doesn't the garden look splendid, Matt?" she'd say before he left.

"Award winning, just like the woman who created it," he'd reply with his big arm around her tiny waist.

Black Friday Revenge

Throngs of shoppers pushed through the barriers at the Roseland, New York, mall on the busiest shopping day of the year. Within two minutes a man suffered a broken nose, a woman dislocated her shoulder, and a teenager suffocated to death under the pile of bodies that formed just beyond the entrance.

Greg Garrison hadn't yet returned from work when he heard the news from a friend who watched it all unfold on live TV. So when the order came down, he knew just what he had to do to avenge his son's death. Next holiday he would lure unsuspecting shoppers into an abandoned warehouse with promises of "deep" discounts and "final" sales. When they all lined up and entered the large steel doors, they would be shut in for good—and the sinister shopping games would commence.

Greg slid open the thick, grimy front door of the three-story warehouse on the corner of 15th and Haywood, just across town from the mall where his son lost his life. He had placed a call back in February to the number on the large "For Lease" sign on the chain-link fence that surrounded the building. For months after that fateful November, he searched for a place large enough to accommodate his plan. It could certainly fit hundreds of shoppers in it at one time. *The tighter, the better*, he thought. He had convinced the property owners, Coleman Properties, that he wanted to hold a fundraising event on Thanksgiving week. For three thousand dollars and a signed agreement to clean up afterward, he was given the key and permission to rent the building for a week. All he needed to do now was set his plan in motion before Black Friday.

Large pulleys and hooks hung from the steel rafters. A flip of a switch proved that several of the idle machines—a conveyor belt, a stretch wrapper, and a ceiling transport lift—were fully operational. Small windowless rooms, which included a walk-in cooler, outlined the edge of the large open space. There was only one other door at the north end of the facility, which he quickly bolted shut. The walls were thick cement, and the windows were high up on the top story, impossible to get to. It was the perfect space.

The day following the previous Christmas, Greg had driven his truck around the city at night and collected empty boxes at the curbs of sleeping residents: boxes for computers, boxes for video game consoles, boxes for children's toys and whatever other intact ones he could find. He flattened and stored them in his garage and basement for nearly a year. As he restored each one in the center of the warehouse, and stacked them high from end to end, he reveled in his preparations.

A week earlier he had large banners made to drape over the boarded-up windows above the main entrance. One read "75% Off Everything." Another promised, "Best Deals in Town." And just below those, a large red banner with white lettering proclaimed: "Shop Till You Drop."

He had placed ads in several of the newspapers for the Grand Opening, which, to follow suit with the other unscrupulous retailers, would begin at 8 p.m. on Thanksgiving Day. Shoppers would need a good meal to sustain what he planned to put them through.

The night before the big day, he strung Christmas lights up in the rafters and adorned the twenty or more hooks with giant colored ornaments. Just inside the entrance, he filled two large barrels with "Magic Sale Bracelets." He placed fake price tags on the boxes, along with "Price Slashing" signs in front of the various stacked groupings. Aisles of more boxes flanked both sides of the large space, concealing the machines behind them. And in the middle of the warehouse, he built a ten-foot-high raised platform out of two-by-fours. This is where he would play Santa and dole out the "rewards."

For the final touch, he wrangled a line of shopping carts from the nearby supermarket that had left them outside the store entrance. Anything to make his "storefront" look real. Then he placed a 60-inch LCD TV screen behind the platform, and added a stereo system with an attached microphone. The large speakers pumped out "Silent Night" on low volume as he completed the warehouse transformation.

As he left the building, Greg thought about how his son never meant to get caught up in the shopping frenzy that ended his life. Danny had stopped in the mall just to pick up a nice tie for his father, not knowing what would unfold once the doors were opened. He never stood a chance. After the first person fell in front of him, the wave of shoppers pushed through like a tsunami. Dozens toppled on top of him, including a 300-pound woman and her 200-pound daughter. His ribcage collapsed and his breath squeezed out of him as he lay covered by bodies, unable to cry out for help. It was a horrendous way to go. Death by discounts.

"Welcome Shoppers!" Greg greeted the first arrivals as early as 6 a.m. Thanksgiving Day. Many had brought tents, which they set up in the large parking lot. By noon there were over fifty asphalt campsites strewn about.

"I can't wait to save money," a woman responded when Greg

asked why she was there so early. "To me, it's *all* about getting the best deals!"

"What about Thanksgiving?" Greg replied.

"I'm sure they'll understand. Especially when they open up their presents on Christmas Day!" The woman returned to her group of friends, who high-fived her just for being a part of the *blessed* event.

By 5 p.m., a crowd of about two hundred people started to form in front of the warehouse entrance. And at 7:55 p.m., the number of shoppers had doubled. Greg grabbed the speaker horn one last time.

"In just five minutes, all of you will have the chance to be the first shoppers at the new Roseland Outlet Store. I know some of you have been waiting patiently in the cold all day long. But I have something special that I think will make you *very* happy. On the other side of this door," he pointed behind him, "you will find two large barrels with Magic Bracelets. Put those on as soon as you get inside, and you will receive an additional fifteen percent off every purchase."

The crowd roared.

"Consider it my gift to you, for coming out."

"I'll take two!" shouted a chubby man in the center of the congregation.

"There are just about enough bracelets for the number of shoppers here, but," Greg hid his smile behind the horn, "if you happen to snag a few more, then, be that as it may."

The crowd began to chant as Greg retreated back inside the warehouse.

"Move that door! Move that door! Move that door!"

At exactly eight o'clock, Greg slid open the massive metal door and the rush of people beelined for the barrels—just as he had planned.

"There they are!" one shouted.

Like the year before, shoppers tumbled on top of each other.

Those who made it to the barrels first quickly snapped the thick, high-tech black bands around their wrists. Several got caught up in tug-of-war battles as supplies diminished. Eventually, though, everyone had acquired a Magic Bracelet. A few put them around their ankles like some sort of fashion statement. Sales chic.

"I got mine!"

"Me too!"

Greg grabbed the microphone from the raised platform and spoke through the speakers. "Everyone inside! Make room for everyone."

The crowd pushed forward within feet of the base of the platform. The final shopper slid the door shut as Greg had commanded.

"When I push this big red button here," Greg pointed to a makeshift button he had rigged in the center of the podium from where he spoke, "shopping will begin!"

The crowd roared again, this time so loud that it echoed off the cement walls and reverberated throughout the warehouse.

"Push it! Push it! Push it!"

"As you wish!" With the chanting of the shoppers, Greg slapped the red button with his left hand. Piercing screams rang out, followed by a loud *thump*, as all four hundred shoppers simultaneously fell to the ground. Their bodies twitched and their eyes widened as if a ghost had just appeared. Greg sauntered down the steps of the platform and walked among them.

"This," he said as he held a remote control with a similar red button in his hand, "is what will happen if you get out of hand. The bracelets you are wearing have no sales power whatsoever. What they do have is the ability to send 50,000 volts of electricity throughout your body. The TSA had wanted them at one time to adorn airline passengers, but when the public outcry over overzealous security nixed the plan, I was able to purchase these taser bands at a mighty-fine discount. Even I," he laughed, "enjoy a good bargain."

Hundreds of shifting eyes followed Greg as he stepped around the fallen.

"Your mind is probably telling your body about now to get up and run, but your nervous system won't have it. Five minutes of incapacitation is what you'll get if you don't follow my commands exactly as I tell you."

The bodies moaned like beached sea lions. Greg stopped beside the chubby man who had requested more bracelets. Foam poured from the man's mouth while his eyes turned up into his head.

"Here's an example of what greed will get you." Greg used a yardstick to push up the dead man's pant leg.

"Count them. One bracelet on each wrist, and one on his ankle. I'm guessing the third one did him in. A forty-five percent price reduction is no match for 150,000 volts. What a shame."

Heavy sighs rippled across the room as the shoppers twisted and turned like newly hit road kill. By the time Greg made it back to the raised platform, some managed to sit up.

"You can't do this to us!" shouted a woman wearing sweatpants and a faded Honey Boo Boo T-shirt.

"I believe I already have. You'll notice that the bands are locked tight around your wrists. Any attempts to take them off, and you'll *all* be brought down again." Greg hovered his hand over the large red button. "I guess it's time you worked together. By the way you all rushed in here, pushing each other out of the way like meth addicts seeking a fix, that might be a challenge."

Greg pointed to the front door.

"There's only one way to exit this enclosure you've found yourself in: the way you came in. You behave, and play the games I have in store for you, and maybe, just maybe, *some* of you will get your freedom."

Greg picked up another remote and turned on the TV behind him.

"First, though, we're going to watch a little TV. This is what happened at the mall across town one year ago this very evening. I'm guessing many of you were there looking to snatch up those bargains, your mouths drooling like animals for $35 off your stupid TVs and your precious game controllers. My son," Greg paused to look around at the startled faces, "my son lost his life because of you. Now watch!"

News coverage from various stations across the country showed the hoards of shoppers trampling over each other. A female CBS reporter spoke with a glimmer in her eyes while the footage looped behind her. "One young teenager, Danny Garrison, was trampled to death when shoppers refused to listen to store attendants to stay back. Police and ambulances arrived on the scene to take others to local hospitals. Is this what Christmas has become?"

"Apparently so." Greg turned off the TV and started the stereo music player. "Santa Claus is Coming to Town" pumped throughout the warehouse. "A little Christmas music to get everyone in the mood?" He snickered and sang along for a moment. "Gonna find out who's naughty and nice..."

By now all the shoppers had risen to their feet.

"Attention, everyone," Greg continued, "I will now divide you into two teams. Those whose last names begin with A through L move to the west side of the warehouse and stand in front of the boxes. The rest of you move to the east side. You have two minutes to do so."

Eyes rife with fear, the shoppers quickly crisscrossed the warehouse like a rush-hour mob at Grand Central Station.

"Okay, our first game is called, appropriately, Shop Till You Drop. There are ten shopping carts on each side of the room. In groups of ten, each team must push those carts to the opposite side and fill them up with as many boxes as possible. Then they must return to their side of the warehouse and stack the boxes against the wall. And," Greg smiled as he peered out among his captive subjects, "just like your precious, real-life shopping sprees, opposing team members can get in the way and hinder your progress."

A collective sigh rang out among the crowd.

Greg continued. "But here you have *additional* weapons at your disposal. You'll notice that each cart has a set of strap-on metal spikes in the basket. Loop those around your cart, if you so wish."

"I'm not doing it," shouted a thug in overpriced sneakers on the east side.

"Do it, or you *all* die." Greg caressed the red button on the podium as if it were an erogenous zone waiting to be stimulated.

"Shut up, kid!" shouted a woman in his group. "You're gonna get us killed!"

"That's right, listen to the lady." Greg returned his hand to the microphone. "She obviously has experience in this sort of thing." He turned and pointed to the large industrial clock on the wall behind him. "When the minute hand hits 8:30 p.m., you'll have twenty minutes to complete your task. You may prepare your carts now."

Shoppers from both sides scrambled for the shopping carts and picked which team members would be the first pushers. All but three carts were rigged with the metal spikes.

"Ten, nine, eight, seven, six..." Greg counted down as the final seconds ticked away. "ONE. SHOP!"

Twenty shopping carts simultaneously raced across the warehouse while hundreds of people on both sides cheered them on. At first the challenge was orderly; the first few carts were allowed to pass through and collect boxes. But as the minutes withered away and the reality set in as to who may lose the race, the game abruptly turned for the worse. Opponents purposely got in the way of each other and forced the carts to collide. Screams of agony and cries for help rose above the din of screeching tires each time a shopper was impaled by the sharp spikes. Waists slashed wide open and blood spurted onto the cement floor, making it wet and slippery. Bodies began to pile up as if a bomb had just exploded. One woman was killed from behind when a spike shot through her back and exited out her stomach. A man was bludgeoned in the face by a cart returning along the path where he had fallen. His left eyeball hung out of its socket by a strand of tissue.

Greg smiled as he witnessed the life-or-death chaos unfold in front of him. It was like a coliseum of carnage. Blood splattered onto the boxes and into the faces of those lucky enough to survive. "What a beautiful Christmas red," he chimed over the loud speakers. Tires ran over wrists and heads. Some shoppers slipped and fell to their deaths, their heads cracking open on the cement. One man suffered a heart attack. When the clock struck 8:50 p.m., Greg grabbed the microphone and spoke to the remaining shoppers.

"Carts down. Return to your sides."

A thick, acrid aroma of fresh blood and sweat filled the air as the teams retreated. Members sought to help other members still clinging to life.

"This is insane!" shouted one of them.

"Yes, it *is* insane, isn't it?" Greg passed his hand in front of him to acknowledge the dead and dying. "But this is all your doing. I didn't push a single cart. Nor did I choose to adorn them with weaponry."

Greg looked to the far east and west walls.

"It looks like the east side team delivered the most boxes back. It takes speed and stamina and determination to achieve such a task. But I'm not sure the price was worth the reward. *You* will be responsible for removing the dead bodies and placing them into the walk-in cooler behind me. The others can clean up the mess. You have ten minutes before our next game. So move!"

Bodies dragged across the warehouse floor, leaving behind waist-wide blood trails. From Greg's vantage point it looked like a giant red finger painting. The dead, and the soon to be dead, were stacked in the back of the cooler four layers high. One thin woman tore in half as she was tossed on top. The remaining shoppers sopped up the drying blood with a couple of mops found in one of the storage rooms. It was a gruesome scene, like the aftermath of a battle of war: one hundred casualties and three hundred shell-shocked.

"Okay, everyone back to the front." Greg grabbed the microphone and commanded the survivors to return. "Our next game is called Stocking Stuffers, or more appropriately," he smiled, "Stockroom Stuffers. Behind me, on opposite sides of the cooler where your comrades are stored, are two 15-foot by 15-foot rooms. You will be divided up again into two teams. The team that can fit the most members into their room within ten minutes will win."

"What do we win?" A bald man in a worn Duck Dynasty T-shirt spoke up while holding a bloodstained cloth around his right hand.

"Your freedom, of course."

"You'll let us go? We can leave?"

"I will open that large door that you came in and you'll be free to walk out. Now," Greg pointed to the center of the warehouse in front of the platform, "line up and divide yourself into two groups. Every other person walk to the opposite storage room and stand in front of it. That will create two groups of roughly one hundred fifty people each. Do it now."

Two equal-sized crowds formed at the north wall. Five minutes later, at precisely 9:30 p.m., Greg gave the call to enter the rooms.

"STUFF yourself!"

Both teams, rather than strategizing on how best to accomplish the task—like removing excess clothing—pushed through the doors like a herd of cattle. Shoulders jarred into each other. Some members fell down inside and never came up. Bodies outlined the back walls and sides like folks seeking

170

personal space inside an elevator, but the centers of the rooms quickly filled in as strangers cramped next to each other.

"MOVE!" shouted a man outside the east room. "We still have half the people outside!"

What seemed like a possibility soon turned into an improbability. Backs pressed firmly against the cement walls, boobs pressed into chests, and genitals pressed into genitals as more people packed in.

"We can do this, people, move closer!"

Chaos broke out in the west room when one woman shouted that she couldn't breathe. The oversized breasts of the woman in front of her soon muffled her screams.

"Sardines!" Greg teased on the mic. "You want your freedom?"

With two minutes left there were still twenty people in front of both rooms. A determined man of bar-bouncer size outside the east room began shoving stragglers through the door.

"Get in, get in!"

"We can't take any more! People are dying in here!" came a voice from the back.

"We can do this! We're almost there!"

One by one, the large man wedged in the remaining members. But his shouts to finish were drowned out by the moans and screams inside. Ribcages cracked under pressure. Eyes bulged out of heads. People pissed their pants. One man's bloodied face pushed into the cement wall until his nose snapped to the side. The death of one person meant more breathing room for the rest, until, eventually, there was no room to breathe at all.

Knowing full well what was going on deep inside, the large man pushed himself between the last two people, creating a vise lock. He was now stuck himself.

"Times UP!"

Greg walked down from the platform and stood inches away from the east room doorway. "You're the winners," he taunted.

"Go ahead now, walk out."

The only movements were gasping heads turning a few degrees from side to side.

"Well, what are you waiting for?"

As he spoke the west team exited their room.

"It seems west has won this time. You don't get your freedom, but you do retain your lives. Come look at this pathetic mess over here. The desire to win at all costs. Again, this was not my doing." Greg directed his comments to the last man in. "I didn't command more people to enter when you could clearly hear the panicked cries of those dying inside. You sacrificed your own team members to win. But in the end, you all lost. Too many fat fucks, I guess. Greed, gluttony. Now you get to die in the stench of your own piss and shit. I can't bear to see this anymore."

Greg slammed the metal door shut. The closing shadow darkened the whites of petrified eyes.

"Now then, where were we?"

A man from the remaining group lunged toward him.

"Andddd. OUT!"

Greg depressed the red button on the remote in his hand and everyone fell to the floor. Their bodies writhed on the warehouse floor like maggots on meat. The smell of burning flesh seeped below the door of the closed stockroom as one hundred fifty tasered bodies in close contact cooked in their own juices.

"I warned you, didn't I?"

Greg grabbed the man's foot and dragged him toward the center of the warehouse.

"I think I'll make you the mascot for our next game. The rest of you can enjoy this time out while I prepare." "I'll be Home for Christmas" played over the loud speakers as if to torment the survivors.

Greg moved the remaining empty boxes to the opposite walls. He placed the man, who was just coming to, on the large turntable of the pallet wrapper, then tucked the loose end of the plastic film around the man's belt loop. The reflection from the machine in operation mirrored off Greg's glasses, the image compressing and stretching as the turntable slowly spun around. Greg marveled at the sight in front of him. It was perfect.

"Everyone," Greg called out to the remaining shoppers, who were now returning to the front of the warehouse.

"Dear God!" one of them cried out.

Hanging up in the rafters from one of the large hooks, balled up inside several layers of thick plastic film, was the man who went astray.

"Are we ready for our next game? I call this one Gift Wrap. As you can see, the previous owners of this warehouse left behind several working machines. This one is called a pallet wrapper. You'll notice that it has a five-foot-diameter turntable at the base, and a vertically traversing arm at one side, which holds industrial-strength clear plastic film on a rotating roller. In production, boxes are placed on a pallet and onto the turntable. With the push of this one button," Greg paused to caress the button labeled START, "the turntable rotates and the boxes are neatly, and tightly, wrapped together for shipment."

The horrified shoppers silently watched.

"Now, here is how this game works. I will ask you questions relating to Thanksgiving and Christmas. If you answer correctly, you will survive this round. If you don't," Greg pointed to the encased man dangling from the hook, "well, you'll join our little friend up there as a warehouse ornament."

A collective gasp resounded.

"I'm going to give you a bit of an advantage, though. This turntable can hold up to five people, giving you more chances to get the right answer. But if you answer incorrectly, you will all be bundled together. So teamwork is key to your survival."

Greg moved back to the machine's control panel.

"I'll take the first group. Come forward."

A pair of women reluctantly stepped onto the turntable. Greg commanded one of them to tie the loose end of the wrap around her waist.

"Our first question: Is Santa Claus from the North Pole or the South Pole? Give me one answer."

The women sighed relief.

"North Pole," said one of them.

"That is correct. You may both step off the turntable and move to the west side of the warehouse. Next group?"

Confident after the first question, two young men immediately jumped onto the turntable.

"Tie the plastic around your belt loop. Your question is: In what state resides the iconic Plymouth Rock?"

The men conferred for a moment before one of them shouted his answer.

"Michigan! Plymouth, Michigan!"

"Wrong. It's Massachusetts. Surely the Mayflower didn't hop over land before coming ashore." Greg slapped the START button and the turntable spun around. One of the men tried to jump off, but the first turn had already bound his legs together. The crowd watched the men's futile struggles. The machine bundled them up like a spider spinning silk around its prey. The final turns stretched plastic over their faces and forever silenced their screams.

Greg lowered one of the rafter hooks with another lever, jammed it into the plastic man-ball, then pulled it to the ceiling. A pulley system transported it to the center of the warehouse.

"Such a beautiful decoration, you think? Next up!"

From then on, groups of five stepped onto the turntable. But the questions increased in complexity, well beyond the intellectual capacity of the shoppers. By midnight, the rafters glistened with multi-colored balls of suffocating shoppers: twenty five-person, one two-person, and the first man bundled. A few of the balls wiggled like cocoons in transformation while those captive inside tried to free themselves. None were successful.

Greg returned to the platform.

"There are now forty-eight of you left. Your next game will test your pricing skills. This should be easy, since you all seem to be so intent on finding a good deal no matter what it costs. Each of you will come up to the raised platform in the middle of the warehouse. You will be asked a question on which purchase is a better deal. If you get it right, you can walk down the other side. Are we ready?"

"What if you answer it wrong?"

"Well then, you aren't so good of a shopper, are you? Now form a line everyone. First up, you in the I'm With Stupid shirt."

A woman in her thirties ascended the steps to the top of the platform.

"Your question is: If an Xbox is on sale at Circuit City for $199, but also sells at Target for $219 with a $10 off coupon, where will you go for the better deal?"

"That's easy, Circuit City."

"Wrong, Circuit City went out of business years ago." Greg pulled a wooden lever and a trap door opened on the floor of the platform. The woman quickly disappeared.

"Next!"

The next person in line reluctantly walked up.

"Your question, sir, is: If the Target on Riverside Drive has a Vizio 32-inch TV on sale for $258, and Walmart on New Grove Avenue by the highway has that same TV for $255, which is the better deal?

The man paused for a second.

"The one at Walmart."

"Wrong. Walmart is 20 miles away, making it a 40-mile round trip. The gas alone would exceed the $3 savings."

Greg pulled the wooden lever again, and the man disappeared.

"Where are they going?" asked I'm With Stupid's other half.

"Oh, just down a chute to Santa's workshop in the basement.

I've hired a math instructor to help them with their shopping skills." This is what Greg told them until the game was over. At two in the morning, he stepped up to the platform and spoke to the remaining five shoppers who correctly answered their questions.

"I've been a little dishonest about the plight of your comrades. I've set up a video camera in the basement of the warehouse so you can see." Greg grabbed the remote and turned on the TV. The survivors gasped at what they saw on the screen.

One after another, the disappearing shoppers had slid into the intake funnel of a giant shredder. Blood shot from their mouths as soon as the metal inner workings grabbed hold of their feet and began to grind them into pieces. Their twisted faces revealed the agony of their demise. Out the other side of the machine, torn colored fabric mixed with chunks of human flesh and spilled into a large bin.

One of the onlookers vomited. Another almost passed out.

"So you see," Greg smiled, "you are the lucky ones." He waved his hand in the direction of the large open warehouse.

"We have one more game to play, and it will decide which of you walks out that door. Your freedom lies in the boxes that you moved about the warehouse in the first challenge. In one of those boxes is a key to unlock your taser band. In another box is a red remote button similar to the one I have up here. The thing is, only one of you can walk free. If you find the key first, the others can fight you for it. It will only unlock one band. If you find the red button first, you can subdue the others while you continue to look. If you find both, well, I'd say you're pretty lucky."

"You're a sick fuck!" shouted one of them.

"Yes, yes I am. Now let's begin. I'm going to start the game out with an initial jolt. When you recover, you can begin your search."

Greg slapped the red button on the platform and all five shoppers fell to the ground. As they twitched, he turned up the holiday music. "Chestnuts roasting on an open fire" played over the speakers.

"Shoppers roasting on a warehouse floor..." Greg crooned along.

The remaining group consisted of three women and two men. The first to rise up from the floor was a man wearing bloodstained jeans and a Justin Bieber T-shirt. He staggered over to the boxes on the west side of the warehouse and began shaking them. Next, two women moved to the east side and immediately tore into the boxes. The final survivors attacked boxes on both sides.

"I found something!" one woman shouted five minutes in. The others abruptly looked up. She struggled to untape the box, using her teeth at one moment. Eventually she gnawed a hole large enough to fit her hand through.

"What is it? The key or the button?" shouted one of the other women.

"I don't know! It feels like some sort of—"

SNAP!

A horrific scream penetrated the pandemonium. The woman pulled out her arm to reveal a bloodied stump where her hand once was. Blood sprayed out of her body and spilled onto the boxes.

"Oh yeah, I forgot to tell you. There are a few other little gifts inside for you. Looks like you found the modified bear trap. I made sure the teeth were extra sharp to cut through flesh," Greg barbed.

By the time the other shoppers realized what had happened, one of the men had opened a box containing a chemical solvent, which quickly ate away at his arm, neck, and chest where it spilled. Once the acid burned through to his carotid artery, blood trickled out of his neck like sap from a tapped maple tree. Within seconds, both the man and the woman collapsed to their deaths.

"And then there were three." Greg laughed and continued to

sing. "Jack Frost nipping at your limbs..."

The remaining survivors carefully opened box after box, until ten minutes later, when one of the women discovered the red button.

"What should I do! What should I do!"

The others ran over to her and pleaded not to press it.

"We can work together! You don't have to do this!"

"But he said there can only be one survivor."

"So we'll all just keep looking for the key."

"But once you find the key, only you can be freed. That leaves the rest of us to die."

On that, the woman depressed the button, not realizing that her own taser band would also be activated. The trio fell to the ground like canaries in a coal mine.

"Wow, you really *are* stupid." Greg laughed as he walked down from the platform and took a few pictures of the knocked-out customers. "You know, a body can only take so much voltage before, well..." He nudged the stiff leg of one of the women with his foot. "Before your heart just stops for good."

All that remained five minutes later were Bieber man and the woman who pressed the button. The man quickly grabbed the remote and resumed his search on the west side. The woman rushed to the east side and climbed a metal ladder to get to the top boxes. Both frantically searched for the taser band key. Twenty minutes later the woman opened a small jewelry box and found the key hidden under the cotton. Her brief silence as she attempted to unlock her band triggered the man to look over. He quickly depressed the red button on the remote. The woman toppled off the ladder and cracked her head on the cement floor, sending the key flying to the middle of the room.

The man twitched on the floor, having shocked himself again. Drool dripped from the corners of his mouth as he slowly dragged himself along the warehouse floor. He hadn't yet regained full use of his hands when he made it to the spot where the key rested. Greg circled around him like a vulture waiting for the final death throes.

"Well, look at you. The winner. Out of all those hundreds of people, you're the only one still alive. A promise is a promise. Let me go open the door for you."

Greg proceeded to pull up the front metal door. A rush of cold air swept into the warehouse.

The man grasped the key with his mouth and stuck it into a small hole in the band. A few seconds later the band popped off. With the numbness subsiding from his legs, he slowly crawled toward the entrance.

"And hey, it's officially Black Friday. So you still have time to shop," Greg teased.

"Fuck you," the man mouthed as he made it out the door and into the dimly light parking lot. The whisks of cars passing along the nearby road attested to his freedom, but the realization was short-lived.

"Oh, and don't forget your cart." One of the rigged carts sailed out of the warehouse and impaled the man in the back just as he was about to stand. The metal spike exited his chest and jutted out of Justin Bieber's mouth.

"Twofers!" Greg retrieved the shopping cart with the dying man still attached and pulled it back into the warehouse, then slid the door down.

For the remainder of the early morning, the final shopper watched as Greg dismantled his platform and sent it and the boxes down the conveyor belt to an outside trash bin. The last images he saw before passing were the anguished faces of the other dead shoppers inside the cooler. A muffled "Silent Night" echoed over the speakers as his eyelids froze open.

Inspection of the warehouse the following Monday was swift. The inspector never checked the stockrooms or cooler, nor bothered to look up into the unlit rafters where one hundred three shoppers were bagged. The plastic had concealed the smell of their decaying bodies. Greg turned over the key and they both left the lot. As they drove away, the "For Lease" sign fell to the ground, ensuring that it would be a long time before anyone would inquire about the abandoned warehouse again.

Somehow the disappearance of the unruly shoppers never garnered much news coverage, nor interest from their families. People who connect more with items than with hearts are seldom missed.

It was a pleasant shopping season that Christmas, and for many years after. There was no pushing, or shoving, or screaming, or tug-of-wars. Shoppers mingled, and smiled, and shared stories about their families as they stood in the short lines. Greg had given the folks of Roseland the best gift ever:

Peace.

Absolute Idiots

Jason Rant stewed in the drive-thru lane at the McDonald's on Oak Street in Kalispell, Montana, while a large, flabby arm from the car in front of him extended toward the intercom. Inside the vehicle silhouettes of several heads bobbed up and down like prairie dogs on the Great Plains. He counted six, graphically confirmed by the six stick-figure decals on the lower left-hand side of the car's rear window. In descending height: dad, mom, big sis, big bro, little sis, and little bro. It was an entire family placing their order.

"Jesus!" Jason yelled out his open window just low enough for the driver not to hear. "You're supposed to go inside if you have a large order! Stupid assholes."

Patience was not a virtue for Jason. He had worked hard all day, and when it came to mealtime, he had no time to dally. Today he was especially hungry, having skipped breakfast to take his car into the shop for new brakes. Three hours of watching CNN and thumbing through year-old tattered magazines in the waiting room left him dry and ravenous. The three cups of coffee brought his blood to a boil.

"Damn you idiots!" Jason seethed as the driver turned back and forth to the children while the attendant repeated each item.

"So that will be two Big Macs, two Happy Meals, one McDouble, Two McChicken sandwiches, four orders of fries, one Diet Coke, two regular Cokes, one Sweet Tea, and two Apple Juice boxes."

"Can you replace one of the McChicken sandwiches with...what do you want? OK, replace it with another McDouble without pickles, and instead of a Coke, I'd like a Sweet Tea as well."

"Will that complete your order?"

"Oh, and can we have...how many? Can we have five Hot Apple Pies, and one McFlurry?"

"What kind of McFlurry?"

"M&M. You want M&M, right? Yeah, M&M."

"OK, will that complete your order?"

"Yes, I think so."

"Okay. Your total is $32.28. Please pull up to the first window."

Jason was about to beep his horn when the driver finally moved forward. But he'd have to wait again. Large orders require a longer time to make.

The solution was simple. And the revenge—sweet. A nighttime job as a drive-thru attendant allowed him to plant special toys inside the giant bags of big orders. Toys that when wound too tightly would spark on recoil and ignite the explosive powder inside. These were not-so-happy meals.

By the fall of 2022, nearly twenty percent of the world's population had been expunged. Most were bad drivers or cell phone addicts. No surprise there. As the World Order Alliance deadline for selective homicides approached—December 31, 2022 being the last day to do the deed—it was all-out bedlam. No applications were required for the final three months. And no one was immune: no race, no color, and no religious sector. Stupidity was an equal opportunity employer. People scrambled to remove the rest of the bad seeds. Seeds that when planted in other seeds would result in more unwanted weeds. And no one wanted to return to the way it was before. Unlike the movie *The Purge*, where victims were chosen at random, there was a reason for these remaining targets: remove the ignorant—the absolute idiots—and achieve worldwide bliss.

Here are a few of those final casualties.

Customer Service Zombies

Denise Roberts had just purchased a 60" smart TV when she realized the darn thing wouldn't connect to her new HD DVD player. Sure it could access all the latest streaming services, but her library of DVDs, ranging from *Avatar* to *World War Z*, demanded to be played as well. What she needed was an HDMI cable. Not included, of course.

On her way back home from work the following day, she stopped in at the local Best Electronics. The far inside wall was a giant grid of televisions from every manufacturer: Sony, Panasonic, Vizio, Samsung, LG, Sharp, and more. All the latest gadgets to go with them—external speakers, sound bars, remote streaming devices—were also on display. A male sales attendant from the department, who looked as though he hadn't changed out of his blue work shirt in a week, popped up in front of her.

"Hi, can I help you?"

"Yes, I need a cable to connect my DVD player to my new TV."

"I'm not sure if we carry those."

"Really? You must. It's called an HDMI cable."

"An HDN...what was it again?"

"HDMI. Surely you know what that is? This is your department, right?"

"Yeah. But I've never heard of that. I don't think we carry those."

Denise was growing increasingly frustrated with customer service. Just the other day she ran out of ink for her printer and drove over to Office Depot to buy more. The sign said "Guaranteed in Stock," but the magenta cartridge for her Epson model wasn't on the shelf. She signaled a sales attendant, who was laughing and joking with three other workers at a nearby video console. The man came over, yet had no idea what the guarantee was.

"We...just don't have it in," he said.

"Well, I can *see* that. But what is the guarantee?"

"I...all I can tell you is that we don't have it in stock."

After she persisted, he finally called his manager from his headset to inform her that they could ship the cartridge to her from their warehouse for free. That was the guarantee. *Shouldn't you have known that?* she thought. In her day you didn't stand around doing nothing. If you weren't helping out a customer, you were learning about the products you were trying to sell.

Back at the electronics store, Denise eventually gave up. She walked up and down the many aisles on her own until she located a slew of HDMI cables in various lengths. She grabbed a six-footer for her TV, then quietly unwrapped a three-footer, walked up behind the dumb sales attendant, and strangled him with it.

"*This* is an HDMI cable, you idiot."

Man Sanitizer

He thought he was going to die. His lungs had filled with fluid, his throat felt as though a sheet of 40-grit sandpaper had rubbed it raw, and his head was so congested he wanted to bash it against the door frame to loosen things up. Trent Gilmore from Essex recounted the previous week of illness to a friend at the Tolinsworth Restaurant.

"Ten days in bed. It was horrible," he said to Jordan as they waited for their entrees. His voice was still a little hoarse.

"And I'm not sure how I got it. I always wash my hands."

It was the N566 strain of influenza that nearly put him into his grave. This one had started in West Africa, where all the world's viruses tended to originate. Highly contagious, they said on the news. Can live on surfaces for up to two days. And once you got it, there was no easy cure. Over-the-counter medications did what they always did: barely alleviate the symptoms for a few hours. Several people in the UK had already died from it. The victims ranged in age from fourteen to seventy.

Before the meal was served, Trent sought out the men's restroom. He had already downed two full glasses of water to compensate for the illness' vestiges. The place was packed that evening, and so were the urinals and stalls. Three other gents waited in line in front of him before he was able to take his shot. In that time he watched the others rapidly pee, flush (sometimes), and bolt for the door. Only two of the seven men stopped at the sink to wash up, and that didn't include the three who exited the stalls and left behind the horrid stench. A few of them coughed into their fists before reaching for the door handle.

Trent stood over the sink and mulled the disgusting behavior he had just witnessed. The lack of hygiene was disgraceful. He lathered his own hands, sang the Happy Birthday song twice in his head like they tell you, then rinsed them clean. *What's the use, really?* he thought. Some guys didn't even use soap, so the faucet knobs were probably contaminated. *If that doesn't get me, it could be the lever for the paper towels. That door handle would be mighty iffy.* He wondered about the cultures crawling on it that very instant. *Another ten days in bed just waiting right there.*

Then he got an idea.

A week later he paired with an adroit comrade at the University of London's Health and Human Sciences School to develop an aerosol spray for the filthy. A sort of Raid for the repugnant that would kill on contact. The contents included a potent sedative, so they'd instantly fall to the ground, and an undisclosed chemical that would suspend their breathing and disintegrate their virus-spewing lungs.

The Escalator

Jake Walstrum was riding down the escalator at the D.C. Metro's Farragut West stop on the morning of November 14, 2022, when the woman in front of him paused at the bottom and just stood there. As he approached, he turned his body sideways, raised his leather briefcase high in the air, then whacked her across the head with it.

Mindless

Margaret and Jackie were having a conversation outside of the Cafe LaCoute in Portsmouth, New Hampshire, when Margaret suddenly realized Jackie knew nothing about what she was talking about. She didn't *get* common idioms, like "two peas in a pod," she never heard of the TV show *All in the Family*, and when asked which country she'd like to visit someday, Jackie replied, "Africa."

"Oh, dear god," Margaret exclaimed, before picking up her butter knife and thrusting it into her friend's neck.

Checkout Time

Gladys Murphy was having a party. She filled her shopping cart to the brim with all the party supplies her local dollar store in Littleton, Colorado, had to offer: party hats, party blowers, party streamers, party balloons, party plates, party cups, party utensils, party name tags, party banners, party candles, and party treats. She *slowly* placed each item onto the checkout conveyor while the cashier *slowly* rang in each item separately. Gladys was holding up the line, and the seven people behind her wanted her dead.

Terry Jones took the lead. He was the one who barred the door shut and held the gun. The six other customers, all who had just a few items to purchase before getting stuck behind party lady and Mr. Slow-Ass cashier, cleared away a spot in the front of the store. It was the place usually reserved for holiday decor and associated products. Halloween was rapidly approaching, so bags of candy and cheap ghoulish items still filled the aisles. In their place they set up a card table, which they had retrieved from the employee storage room, and surrounded it on all four sides with six-foot-high shelves. No one from outside the store could see what was about to take place.

Gladys, Dan the checkout man, Tom the stock boy, and manager Belinda sat quietly in opposite chairs with their hands tied behind their backs. Quietly because all four had been gagged with duct tape (located on aisle 4) before being pushed up to the table. Terry circled around them while waving his pistol. The four captives watched in horror.

"What brought you here today is simple. You are our honored guests. And *we* are going to have a party." Terry paused next to Gladys. "Lady, you like parties, don't you?" He grazed the side of the thirty-year-old soccer mom's face with the cold barrel of his gun. She tried to turn away. He bent over and whispered in her ear. "I like parties, too, mama." Gladys gave him a cold look.

"But why," Terry stood up and continued walking around the table, "why was it necessary for you to purchase so many items at one time? Three hundred and twenty-one, from what we counted as we waited behind you for nearly twenty minutes." He stopped opposite from her. "Efficiency? Get it all in one swoop? Cover your list and be done with it?" Gladys met his eyes again. "The problem with that, you see, is you neglected to think about the other people around you. Maybe you should have made it a few trips, or divided it up and returned to the checkout."

Terry leaned against one of the shelves while the helpers proceeded to load them back up with bags of candy.

"Common courtesy. Common courtesy. Where the hell has common courtesy gone?"

Terry proceeded around the table to Dan, whose name was stitched onto his work shirt.

"Danny boy, Danny boy. Where do I begin with you? That speed in which you checkout customers. What is that? First gear? Maybe second? Or is it neutral?" Terry positioned himself directly behind the man and pressed the tip of the gun under his chin. Dan groaned and his eyes watered. "Ahhhh. Perhaps this would get you to work a little faster. Under the gun, so to speak." Terry laughed. "Like, was it necessary to pass each of this fine lady's items over the scanner one at a time? Could you not have counted the number of similar items, then keyed in a quantity and a single price?"

Bang!

A bag of Tootsie Pops fell to the ground, making everyone think the gun had gone off. Dan began to weep. Terry continued.

"Is this your way of punishing the customers? We get it. You hate your job. But don't take it out on us. Speed is of the essence. Speed is what makes us happy. Need for speed, Dan. Need for speed."

By now two of the four shelves had been filled with layers and layers of sweet treats: Tootsie Rolls, Tootsie Pops, Smarties, Hershey Bars, Milky Ways, Whoppers, Reese's Pieces, candy corn, candy pumpkins, scary eyeballs, blow pops, wax bottles, wax lips, and Twix. Terry made his way over to stockboy Tom.

"And my friend, where were you when we were in line?" Terry rested the gun on the lad's right shoulder so the kid could see the barrel out of the corner of his eye. "On a *smoke* break? Isn't that where you always are? In the back somewhere. Outside checking your smartphone for messages, perhaps? Certainly not up front *where you were needed the most*. Tell me, does that work for you? Evading your job. Dawdling. Hiding down some aisle rearranging products over a ten-minute period that you could have tackled in two? Why even think of helping out your friend Dan here. After all, that would mean *working*."

Terry cocked the gun. The four jolted. Terry smiled and moved over to the store manager.

"Hey? How's it goin', sweet cheeks?" He leaned against her chair so his knees pushed into her bound hands. "I see you're *special*. You have on a white shirt while the others wear green. You know what that means, don't you? It means you have *responsibilities*. And one of those responsibilities is making the customers happy. And one of the ways to make the customers happy is to not make them wait." Terry pressed the gun against the woman's left temple. "But you thought it was better to sit up there in your little office cubicle and feign office work. Looking out of that two-way glass window and seeing how impatient we were growing. Watching the line snake around the battery endcap and down aisle eight. For all you knew, there could have been thirty of us. Exactly how long were you going to wait before you called stock boy here up front? Or come down from your mighty loft and open an additional checkout lane? And even if you did, I *know* your little secret." Terry leaned into her and whispered. "You keep the light off so people won't think you're really open. You'd only be there *temporarily* to do us a *favor*. Why give the impression that you want to help? Why burden yourself with...the customers?"

Terry raised the gun overhead and shot a single bullet. Tiny particles from the drop-ceiling panel snowed down like white confetti.

"It's party time!"

The six co-conspirators had filled the surrounding shelves with all the candy in the store. Terry walked around the table and slipped a party cap on each of the four. He followed with glow-in-the-dark loops around their necks (aisle 2). One of the women placed a large plastic bowl in the center of the table. Another filled it with several bags of chocolate treats. Terry freed up the victims' hands, but secured their legs and bodies to the chairs with nylon rope (aisle 3). Then he violently ripped the tape off their mouths while pressing his gun to their heads should they attempt to scream.

"Here's how it works. You will eat candy. You will eat candy until all of this candy surrounding you is gone. If you don't finish, you will get a bullet to the head. It's that simple. And I don't want to hear a peep from you. The customer's always right!" He laughed.

It was nine o'clock on that late-October evening. By then all the neighboring stores had closed up. The overhead clock ticked away while mouths chewed and wrappers fell to the floor. Two hours went by. Stomachs bulged. Insulin levels rose. Diabetic shock took out one of them. Another got a Tootsie Pop lodged inside his throat. Dan the checkout man ate so much his lap band snapped. Internal bleeding was his end.

But Gladys, the woman who started it all, kept on chewing. She had consumed four bags of Reese's Pieces, ten Hershey Bars, three bags of candy corn, and eighteen wax juice bottles before pausing to vomit it all up. Then she continued, which surprised everyone.

"I have a party to go to," she said with a chocolate-covered grin before reaching for the stack of Twix minis. "And I *don't* intend to miss it."

Gladys would survive.

Other Reads by Victor Rook

In Search of Good Times
Joseph Manley, a blue-collar worker from Idaho, loses his job during the 2009 economic recession. A strange turn of events sets him off on a road trip to seek out the fictional sitcom families from "Good Times" and "All in the Family." Haunted inns, abandoned houses, catastrophic weather, quirky couples, gangs, hippies, soldiers, loving dads, strong mothers—even an intuitive stray dog await Joe on his journey. Will he find the Evans and Bunker families—or something else? (224 pp.) Available on Amazon.com.

Musings of a Dysfunctional Life
Bringing clarity and understanding to our own dysfunctional lives, award-winning filmmaker Victor Rook recounts his childhood, teenage, and middle-aged years through both humorous and poignant recollections. These short stories cover life's gamut: dreams, sex, innocence, religion, music, pets, ghosts, aging, and more. (214 pp.) Available on Amazon.com.

PEOPLE WHO NEED TO DIE

34628703R00114

Made in the USA
Charleston, SC
13 October 2014